Jase wasn't sure who made the last small move that brought them together.

Melanie's soft lips tasted like sweet papaya. An odd, exhilarating feeling hit him like a lightning bolt out of nowhere and sent his head spinning. He wanted to sink into her sweetness, to take her up—here and now—on everything she was reluctantly offering.

Jase pressed closer and licked the corner of her lips. Melanie gave a soft, startled sigh, but didn't move back. If anything, she leaned toward him. Hot need plowed through him like a freight train.

In the back of his mind he was aware of the open door. He knew if someone walked by, it would mean instant execution. They'd drag him outside and shoot him like a dog. He *was* a dog, for taking advantage of her like this.

Yet with Melanie's lips on his, the guilt and the risk didn't seem so grave, and certainly seemed worth it....

DANA MARTON

SPY HARD

TORONTO NEW YORK LONDON
AMSTERDAM PARIS SYDNEY HAMBURG
STOCKHOLM ATHENS TOKYO MILAN MADRID
PRAGUE WARSAW BUDAPEST AUCKLAND

If you purchased this book without a cover you should be aware that this book is stolen property. It was reported as "unsold and destroyed" to the publisher, and neither the author nor the publisher has received any payment for this "stripped book."

This book is dedicated to Cindy Whitesel and Amy Ignatz, friends I've been lucky enough to reconnect with lately.

With my sincere thanks to Allison Lyons.

Recycling programs for this product may not exist in your area.

ISBN-13: 978-0-373-69625-3

SPY HARD

Copyright © 2012 by Dana Marton

All rights reserved. Except for use in any review, the reproduction or utilization of this work in whole or in part in any form by any electronic, mechanical or other means, now known or hereafter invented, including xerography, photocopying and recording, or in any information storage or retrieval system, is forbidden without the written permission of the publisher, Harlequin Enterprises Limited, 225 Duncan Mill Road, Don Mills, Ontario M3B 3K9, Canada.

This is a work of fiction. Names, characters, places and incidents are either the product of the author's imagination or are used fictitiously, and any resemblance to actual persons, living or dead, business establishments, events or locales is entirely coincidental.

This edition published by arrangement with Harlequin Books S.A.

For questions and comments about the quality of this book please contact us at Customer_eCare@Harlequin.ca.

® and TM are trademarks of the publisher. Trademarks indicated with ® are registered in the United States Patent and Trademark Office, the Canadian Trade Marks Office and in other countries.

www.Harlequin.com

Printed in U.S.A.

ABOUT THE AUTHOR

Dana Marton is the author of more than a dozen fast-paced, action-adventure, romantic-suspense novels and a winner of a Daphne du Maurier Award of Excellence. She loves writing books of international intrigue, filled with dangerous plots that try her tough-as-nails heroes and the special women they fall in love with. Her books have been published in seven languages in eleven countries around the world. When not writing or reading, she loves to browse antiques shops and enjoys working in her sizable flower garden, where she searches for "bad" bugs with the skills of a superspy and vanquishes them with the agility of a commando soldier. Every day in her garden is a thriller. To find more information on her books, please visit www.danamarton.com. She loves to hear from her readers and can be reached via email at DanaMarton@DanaMarton.com.

Books by Dana Marton

CAST OF CHARACTERS

Jase Campbell—SDDU commando soldier working undercover in the South American jungle. His information-collecting mission is jeopardized when he meets a powerful drug lord's sister-in-law and falls in love with her.

Melanie Key—Kept captive at a drug lord's jungle camp, Melanie's only wish is to escape. But can she trust Jase? On the surface, he's just another thug, yet he seems more than what meets the eye. He'll be either her salvation or the biggest mistake she's ever made.

SDDU—Special Designation Defense Unit. A top secret commando team used by the U.S. government for clandestine missions abroad, and to track and capture terrorism suspects on U.S. soil.

Don Pedro—The head of a sizable drug cartel, the don is struggling with holding on to power, while trying to expand his business into human smuggling and weapons trade.

Cristobal—Once the don's trusted captain, he is ready to take over his empire of crime, no matter the cost.

Mochi—A child of the jungle, Mochi lost everything to the drug wars.

Chapter One

Lazy drops drummed a unique rhythm on the emerald
leaves. Not rain—not yet, just the humid air weeping in
the South American rain forest. Ripened fruit dropped
from the mango trees, one nearly hitting a capuchin
monkey. The animal jumped aside with a shriek, which
sent a flock of parrots flying from the canopy, red-blue
wings flapping. The soft and harsh noises blended into
perfect harmony, pulsing with life—the morning song
of the jungle.

A few hundred yards to the east, boots splashed in
the shallow water of the ravine. Guns clinked against
the water canteens on the men's hips. The intruders
must not have heard the jungle's music, because they
didn't even try to fit in, creating disharmony.

Mochi perched halfway up the kapok tree, his feet
dangling a hundred feet above the jungle floor. He'd
sneaked out of the village at dawn to spy on the new
batch of baby monkeys, hoping to spot one without a
mother, an orphan he could take home. Since a jaguar
had stolen his pet dog in the spring, the mud hut where
he lived with his three mothers seemed empty.

But the monkeys dashed off the moment those boots
came too close for comfort. Slow minutes passed before

the six men came into view, then stopped to rest right below Mochi. He stayed to see what they were about, even if his mothers would be awake by now and looking for him. When he got home, nothing would save him from a good beating. He bristled at that. Nobody seemed to appreciate that *he* was now the man of the family.

An accident at the diamond mine up north had killed his father three months ago, the same week that his oldest brother had been shot by the drug lord who controlled their village. His three middle brothers had been taken more recently by a curse from an angry jungle spirit one of them had stepped on accidentally. A potion from the witch doctor could have helped, but the witch doctor had been on his annual pilgrimage. So the spirit-curse disease spread through the family, nearly taking Mochi, too. The witch doctor had come back in time to save him, but he'd been too late for the others.

He was still weak and now hungry. A line of lemon ants marched up the trunk not far from him. Not much, but enough to take the taste of hunger out of his mouth. He stood on the wet branch to reach them, balancing on bare feet.

He would never have slipped if a small part of the jungle spirit's curse wasn't still wedged somewhere inside him, making his legs unsteady. He grabbed the branch, his feet scrambling in the air for only a second before they found purchase. He barely made any noise at all. But one of the intruders below looked up, right at him.

A dark smile spread on the man's face.

He weighed the mango in his hand, then threw it hard. The missile hit Mochi square in the middle of his chest, and the boy lost his perilous perch in the tree.

A KID WAS the dead-last thing Jase Campbell needed in the middle of this particular undercover op. He swore under his breath as he watched the boy drop. The soft leaf carpet and the kid's age, meaning flexibility, saved him from any broken bones, as proven by his quick recovery and dash into the trees.

Most of the men were too tired or too lazy to do anything about it. Mercenaries of the biggest crime lord in the area, they were returning to camp after a weeklong trek through the jungle, tired and sweaty. They just wanted to sit for a second and grab a bite to eat.

"¡Alto!" But Alejandro, having gotten the kid out of the tree, took off after him.

Which left Jase no choice but to follow. Not that he knew what he could do without blowing his cover.

He watched where he stepped as he ran. Even a small scratch from a broken shaft of bamboo could cause a fatal infection out here; the bite of a poisonous snake would mean near-instant death. He didn't have to look up to know which way Alejandro went. The idiot made enough noise for a deaf man to follow—first with his feet, then with his wheezing. He'd had way too much palm wine the night before.

"I got it." Jase passed him when the man slowed to catch his breath.

There had to be a village around somewhere, one that wasn't on their itinerary. The kid couldn't have been more than six years old, wouldn't wander into the woods on his own farther than a couple of miles. The boy ran a lot quieter than Alejandro, his tan skin and drab loincloth blending into his surroundings. Only the screeching birds above betrayed the direction he took.

"Hey," he yelled. Not to make the boy stop, but to scare him into running faster.

Trees became sparser, the undergrowth thicker as Jase followed. Soon he came out onto a well-worn trail. Probably led to the boy's village. The kid would reach home safely following it. Jase looked after the boy for a second, then turned back. Time to return to the others and let them mercilessly make fun of both him and Alejandro for being so old and feeble that a child could outrun them.

But he barely walked ten yards before a high-pitched shriek of terror stopped him. He spun on his heels and darted down the trail after the boy.

He expected some sort of an animal attack, but soon he could smell smoke. Then the village came into view—about two dozen primitive dwellings, the huts burned, bodies littering the ground.

He slipped his rifle off his shoulder and waited a few seconds. Nothing moved. He stepped into the clearing and followed the shrieking to a partially burned hut. Inside, the boy kneeled next to a dead woman, tears streaming, leaving shiny tracks on his dirty face. Another woman lay facedown in the back of the hut. The smell of death and smoke hung in the air.

"Take it easy, I'm not going to hurt you."

Every cell of him protested the senseless destruction as Jase reached for the wrist of the woman nearer to him, then the other's. Neither had a pulse. Anger burned in his gut. The wanton murder of innocent villagers was a good reminder of why he did the work he did—to stop tragedies like this from happening. The crime lords of the area considered the locals disposable pawns in their games, and gave even less thought to the countless victims of the drugs and guns they sent north on a regular basis.

"Come on." He grabbed the boy by the arm and pulled him outside before the smoldering roof could collapse on them.

A third woman's lifeless body sprawled behind the hut, the sight sending the kid into a renewed fit of crying.

"Para," he told the boy. *Stop.* Then pushed the kid behind him. Someone was coming.

Alejandro burst from the jungle. "What the hell happened here?" he asked in rapid Spanish.

"Cristobal is pushing his boundaries forward," Jase responded in the same language.

Alejandro's facial muscles tightened as he raised his gun to the sky to squeeze off a jungle telegram.

Jase lifted his hand to hold him off. "Those bastards can't be too far. The huts are still burning."

Alejandro nodded and lowered his weapon. "Better take the news back to Don Pedro as fast as we can. I'll go tell Lucas."

If Cristobal's men were pillaging through this corner of the jungle—a group that likely outnumbered Jase's small team judging by the damage they'd wrought here—their best bet was not to engage them but to take information to Don Pedro instead. The big boss could then decide how he wanted to respond to Cristobal, an ex-captain of his who'd recently turned against him.

Alejandro ran off with a scowl on his pockmarked face.

Jase waited until the man disappeared from sight before turning to the kid.

"Go to the other village." He pointed east.

The small collection of huts they'd left the previous morning was a day's trek for the adults, would be only slightly more for the kid. The boy should be safe there. Cristobal's men weren't heading that way. Jase and the others would have met them if they had been.

He stepped back into the smoldering hut and grabbed some fruit that had been spilled to the ground, took a piece of cloth to wrap the food, then added his canteen to the bundle. "Here."

The boy wouldn't move an inch.

He shoved the kid gently in the right direction.

The boy stepped two feet away, then stopped and stared at him expectantly.

"¡Vamos!"

Might as well have been talking to a wild fig tree.

He turned his back on the boy and moved toward the jungle, hoping the kid would understand that the both of them needed to get going.

But instead of heading for relative safety, the kid followed him.

"You can't come with me," he said in Spanish, having no idea if the kid spoke that language or some isolated native tongue. A day's trek in the jungle to the nearest village would be perilous for the boy, but a day's trek in the jungle with a team of seasoned killers would be even worse.

The kid knew the jungle. With some luck, he had a chance to reach the village. But if he went to Don Pedro's place on the river, his life wouldn't be worth a damn thereafter.

"Run for it." Jase put on a scary face and stomped his foot.

But instead of taking off, the boy began crying again,

which made him feel like a heartless bastard. Which he was, by the way, so he didn't fully understand why his conscience would choose this moment to have a fit.

"Go," he said again, his tone suspiciously close to pleading.

But Alejandro reappeared from the jungle, followed by the other four, and the boy's options disappeared.

The team spread through the village, looking for evidence of Cristobal's men and picking out whatever they wanted to take. No sense in waste.

Alejandro came for the kid.

Jase stepped between them in a stance that would allow him action no matter which way he needed to move.

"I saw him first." The man put his hands on his hip.

His protest drew the others' attention. Lucas strolled closer. As team leader, he was responsible for settling trouble.

Jase being the latest addition to the group, he ranked lowest, firmly on the bottom of the pecking order. He didn't have enough influence to take what he wanted, and to show weakness by admitting that he wanted to save the boy would make the others suspicious. It would conflict too much with the killer image he'd been taking care to cultivate.

"I looked into his dead mother's eyes. Her spirit said it'll curse me if I don't take care of the kid." He nodded toward the charred hut with a grave face.

Lucas moved on. Jungle superstition was its own thing. Nobody went against it.

Alejandro kept the scowl on his face. "Don Pedro would pay me a hundred dollars for him."

Unlikely. Maybe twenty, if Don Pedro needed someone to help out around the dog-fighting rings he ran in the larger towns downriver, or another runner, or a jungle spy—all jobs with a very low life expectancy.

Jase pulled his second-best knife, the one with the serrated double edge that Alejandro had coveted from the beginning, and held it out on his palm.

The man accepted it with a shrug as if being generous, as if the knife wasn't worth ten times more than what he could have gotten for the boy.

"Hey, Jase found himself a little brother," he called out to the rest, and joined in their laughter as he loped off, not wanting to miss any of the scavenging.

The men thought of the forest-dwelling natives as little more than animals, so calling one Jase's brother was an insult. Like calling him stupid, which he was. He risked a multimillion-dollar mission almost a year in the making for a scrawny kid.

He shook his head, then squatted in front of the boy and pointed at himself. "Jase." Then lifted his eyebrows and pointed at the latest complication in his life. Now he would have the responsibility to protect the kid at the compound, and find a way to get him out of this godforsaken corner of the jungle to safety, the sooner the better.

"Mochi." The boy wiped his tears with the back of his dirty little hand.

Jase rubbed the bridge of his nose then looked at the men picking through the village. Rough and tough killers, every one of them. On some level, he wasn't much better. He'd certainly seen and caused plenty of violence over the years. What on earth was he going to do with a kid? It'd be a miracle if his cover wasn't blown and they both survived the day.

THE LAST LEG of the trek back to camp had exhausted the men. They sat around the beaten-up table in the kitchen at the back of the barracks half asleep, taking their last puffs of smoke, their last swigs of the homemade tequila that was being passed around. Night had settled on the jungle around them, thick and dark, exhaustion pulling them toward their bunks in the barracks.

"I need to talk to Alejandro," Lucas said, and nodded toward Jase. "See if he's up at the house."

That got his attention and woke him up. A seal of approval. He'd never been sent up to the house before, not once since he'd joined Don Pedro's empire of crime two months ago. But now it seemed he'd proven himself with the weeklong trek through the jungle and his assistance with the collection of debts.

Plus, he'd discovered the burned village—important intelligence. He'd fully gained Lucas's trust at last, which brought him one step closer to Don Pedro himself, one step closer to crucial information on his operations and business associates.

He glanced at Mochi, who slept on a rug by the woodstove. The women who were responsible for feeding the men had taken care of him. He'd made it through the day, but how long his good luck would continue remained a question. The sooner Jase found a way to get him to another village the better.

He finished his yerba maté and stood to lumber off into the darkness, up to the house where Don Pedro kept his most nefarious secrets.

Sharp voices, men arguing in the barracks, wafted through the night air. A dog barked in the distance. The compound that housed Don Pedro's army of criminals teemed with life, yet Jase felt alone in the middle of it all.

Trust no one. Don't let your guard down for a single second. Those were the top two keys to his survival at the moment. *Don't get involved on a personal level* would have been a good third, but he'd shot that to hell when he'd taken on Mochi this morning.

The downstairs windows of Don Pedro's jungle hacienda were dark. The only light came from upstairs, from Don Pedro's private living quarters—strictly off-limits to all but his closest confidants. Even Lucas wasn't allowed up there. Since Cristobal's attack on his life at his old jungle headquarters, the Don had become paranoid.

Jase slowed as he passed the building he'd observed so many times from afar. He knew every door, every window, every man who was allowed in. He had a plan. And now that he could freely move around the compound, he would be able to implement his plans, slowly, carefully, over the upcoming days.

He glanced up at the balcony and caught a dark shape that didn't quite blend into the rest of the shadows. His hand inched toward his weapon as he moved closer.

A single shot.

One shot could take out the Don right now. The man was responsible for over 10 percent of the drugs and illegal weapons that reached the U.S. Credible intelligence indicated that he was also providing weapons for terrorist cells and was possibly involved in a plan to smuggle terrorists across the U.S. border.

Except, even if he died right now, tonight, someone else would take his place by next week. Someone like Cristobal.

So Jase's orders didn't include assassination. He was to come away with a chart of Don Pedro's organization. They needed to know how he was linked to the other major crime lords in the area, what local cops and higher-up politicians were on his payroll, and who his connections were to those terrorist cells he was rumored to be negotiating with.

Jase's team—the Special Designation Defense Unit—had gained important documents last year. The notebook they'd acquired held crucial information, but not enough. Colonel Wilson wanted more before he launched a serious offensive. As big as Don Pedro was, he was just the first loose thread. Jase had to tug gently, and if he did it right he might just unravel the whole tapestry of corruption and violence.

He had a bug hidden in the lining of his left boot, meant for the Don's office.

As he moved forward through the shadows, the moon peeked from behind the clouds at last and illuminated the figure on the balcony. Long hair framed an oval face, spilling down slim shoulders. Not Don Pedro, after all.

A woman.

Her light hair framed Western features, definitely not Hispanic or a mixture of Hispanic and native, like most of the people on the compound. The hauntingly beautiful face caught Jase off guard. Of course, Don Pedro never settled for anything but the absolute best. He could afford it.

Looking at something pretty felt good after the gruesome massacre he'd seen today. Jase slowed. Then he caught himself and moved along. The last thing he needed was a shot in the head for ogling the boss's girlfriend.

Since the downstairs windows were dark, Alejandro clearly wasn't in the house. Jase strode toward the packaging facility behind the hacienda and scanned the men who stood around up front, but didn't see Alejandro among them, either. He did spot Don Pedro, however. Since he couldn't afford to miss any opportunities to get closer to the boss, he walked forward.

The men were standing in a circle, surrounding Paulo, a burly guy of about forty who usually worked with the runners.

"Where is the missing kilo?" Don Pedro asked in Spanish, his eyes filled with pure menace.

"I swear I didn't touch it. I don't touch what's yours. I never have." The man's voice shook.

The Don nodded to the thug who held Paulo's arm, and the guy planted his fist into Paulo's stomach hard enough to make him double over.

"All I want is that kilo back," the Don said in a deceptively mild tone.

But the accused knew the boss wanted a lot more— his blood and life, in fact. Everyone knew Don Pedro didn't forgive. He didn't believe in setting a bad precedent.

So Paulo went for it, coming up swinging. Since they were all standing together and Don Pedro among them, nobody dared to squeeze off a shot. The men froze for a moment, unsure of what to do, which Jase used to his advantage.

He lunged forward and tackled Paulo to the ground, ignoring the forty or so pounds the man had on him.

Others moved to get in on the action, but a word

from Don Pedro called them back, even as he nodded to Jase to go ahead.

Raw violence went from zero to a hundred in the first second. Paulo fought for his life, while Jase fought for a promotion. He needed to move up in the ranks to get closer to the Don.

The knee to his stomach almost made him lose his dinner. He responded with an elbow to the chin. They rolled in the dust like savages, looking for an opening, a handhold, anything. Paulo had probably been sitting around camp all day, while Jase's body felt every mile of their long trek, his muscles achy, his energy exhausted. He didn't let that stop him.

His eyebrow split from a headbutt as they fought on, then his lips split from a punch the guy had somehow gotten in. He tasted blood and saw stars.

Flipped the man.

The good thing with big ones was that they usually tired faster, since they had to move all that weight. Paulo had never heard of that rule, it seemed. He rolled right over Jase, making his ribs crack and pop under the pressure. But Jase rose and got the upper hand at last, got the man in a headlock and immobilized him. They were both bleeding and breathing hard, nearly choking on the dust-filled air they desperately tried to suck in.

Jase looked over his shoulder at the Don just as the boss nodded to one of his lieutenants, who was holding a gun on Paulo.

The bullet grazed Jase's cheek on its way to slamming into his opponent's head.

He dropped the suddenly limp body to the ground, then pushed to his feet, trying to avoid the growing pool of blood. He looked back at the Don, hoping the man would at least ask his name. But the boss was already walking away.

He didn't give his men orders to clean up the mess; he simply expected it to be done. Two of them were already grabbing Paulo by the feet to drag him away.

A third man, Roberto, clapped Jase on the shoulder. "Want to come over to the fire for some whiskey?"

He was one of the Don's inner circle, not a bad friend to make. But not tonight. Jase couldn't afford to anger his immediate boss by making him wait too long.

"Lucas sent me up for Alejandro. I better find him and get him back to the kitchen," he told the man, and limped back the way he came.

If Alejandro was up this way, he would have come out for the fight. And if he wasn't at the packaging building, he was most likely either with the dogs or the mules.

Jase passed by the main house again, giving it another careful look as he walked. He would come up in the morning and ask for Paulo's job. He'd be turned down with a scoff, but all he needed was an excuse to get inside, see exactly where the office was located.

The woman stood on the balcony in the same spot as before. Something glinted on her face. Sure looked like tears. As the wind changed, he could hear her soft whisper.

"Dear God, please help me away from this place before he kills me. I beg you, please, please send someone to save me." She had a slight Texas accent.

Her words were so filled with desperation they twisted even his stone-cold heart. He kept his gaze on her. So they were both Texans. He told himself that didn't mean they had any sort of connection.

She was the spoiled girlfriend of a murderous criminal, probably upset because she didn't get as many diamonds this week as she'd expected. Sounded like she'd had a fight with Don Pedro earlier. None of Jase's business.

Suddenly she turned his way and peered into the shadows, alarm ringing in her voice as she asked, "Who's there?"

He stepped forward. "Sorry if I bothered you. I'm Jase. I'm looking for one of the men."

She shrunk back.

And he realized what he must look like, fresh from a fight, with blood on his shirt and face, violence still hanging around him in the air. "Sorry." He turned to go.

"Wait," she called after him. "Are you the one who brought that little boy in?"

He raised his gaze back to her. Her large eyes watched him carefully from above a straight, pert nose.

"Consuela from the kitchen told me," she said.

He swore silently. Consuela talked too much. "Scrawny little thing." He gave a dismissive gesture. "I don't think we'll see much work out of him. He might not even make it."

Her face turned even sadder, if possible, the corners of her full lips turning down. She nodded and walked inside the house without looking at him again.

She wasn't what he'd expected from the Don's girlfriend. Although Jase could only see her from the chest up—the wooden railing hid the rest—she looked more like a schoolteacher than a Brazilian photo model, which was Don Pedro's usual entertainment, if the rumors around camp were true.

This one looked wholesome and fragile, completely

inappropriate for the Don. How in hell did someone like her find her way to a place like this?

Clearly a mistake. A mistake she was rapidly realizing, judging by her whispered prayer. Well, he couldn't help her with her troubles. His hands were plenty full already. She'd be nothing but a distraction. And a distracted undercover operative was a dead undercover operative.

He moved on. Dogs barked in their enclosures. The river rushed on in the distance. He didn't take a dozen steps before Alejandro materialized from the darkness.

The man's eyes narrowed with suspicion. "What are you doing here?"

"Lucas sent me to find you."

"You shouldn't be hanging around the house." His voice dripped with disapproval. He puffed his chest out as if he wasn't just another lackey, one measly step above Jase.

"I thought you might have gone up to play cards with the guys in packing."

"Shot the dice with the idiots at the stables." His grim look said he didn't win. "Jorge got back. Says he saw another burned village to the south. Cristobal is definitely heading this way."

Which meant there would be a major battle in a couple of days.

"We'll take care of him." Jase squared his shoulders in a macho display for Alejandro's sake. But his mind was on the boy. He needed to get Mochi out of here at the first opportunity.

He tried not to think of the crying woman whose sad eyes haunted him.

Chapter Two

The woman on the balcony came to him in his sleep. Naked. The dark jungle whispered its mysterious song around them. Silver moonlight splashed on her skin, her long hair tumbling to her waist.

Jase's body turned hard with need, but for some reason he couldn't reach for her. Then he saw at last what held him back. Thorny vines tied him to a tree. He watched, unable to move, as a black jaguar stole forward from the bushes and crouched, getting ready to lunge at the woman. Blood glistened on the animal's muzzle. And as Jase looked around, he could see a small foot sticking out from under the bush where the jaguar had come from. *Mochi.*

He woke to shouting outside the barracks, cold sweat covering his body. Sunlight filtered through the burlap curtains. Lucas rushed in, an extra belt of bullets swung over his shoulder, a scowl on his face.

"What is it?" Jase grabbed his gun first, his shirt second.

"We're preparing for battle. Cristobal sent a messenger. He demands unconditional surrender."

A glance out the window revealed a man lying in the dust on his back behind one of the jeeps. A familiar knife protruded from his throat, the very one that Jase had traded for Mochi. Alejandro was always eager to score points.

"And that would be the messenger?"

Lucas flashed a ferocious grin and rushed on out the back door. Jase washed his face then followed after him, heading to the kitchen to see about the kid and get some coffee. Then he would go straight to the main house. The Don would be calling his people today, needing all his alliances to back him in the battle. Now was a better time than ever to plant that bug. They could gain some serious intelligence out of this.

He strode through the long building he bunked in that resembled the Indian longhouses, a half wall of bamboo erected here and there for privacy. In other places colorful horse blankets hung from the ceiling to separate the bunks from each other. In general, the men didn't much care about their lodgings. Anything was better than sleeping in the open jungle, at the mercy of the elements and the animals.

He pushed through the door into the kitchen, which was little more than a large shack attached to the barracks. But he found the blanket Mochi had slept on empty.

Before he could have gotten worried about the kid, the boy walked in through the back door, chewing on a large chunk of flatbread. The woman from the balcony last night stepped in right behind him, a hand on her round, pregnant belly the railing had hidden the night before.

"Sorry, I'm—" She froze at the sight of Jase. Unease widened her big, thick-lashed Bambi eyes, the color of dark chocolate with gold specs that somehow made them mesmerizing. She pressed her full lips together as she drew back. She'd probably thought all the men were outside and had expected only Consuela in the kitchen.

Once again, she saw him at his worst. His hair hadn't met up with his comb yet this morning; his face hadn't seen a razor in a week. He was unkempt and half-naked… And he couldn't believe he was worrying about his *looks,* for heaven's sake.

He shrugged into his wrinkled shirt and ran his fingers through his hair. "Can I help you?"

It behooved anyone to be nice to the boss's girlfriend.

The boss's *pregnant* girlfriend.

She looked five or six months along. So much for those slim hips in his dream. Not that she looked any less sexy just the way she was. Her full lips captured his attention for a few seconds before his gaze dropped to her breasts that stretched the thin material of her strappy dress. His body instantly responded to her.

Suicidal much? the voice of reason asked in his head. For once in his life, he resolved to listen to it.

"Where are this boy's parents?" Her voice sounded like home.

He would have lied if he said her slight Texas twang didn't affect him. Her large, dark eyes were ringed with shadows, as if she hadn't gotten much sleep lately. None of his business. He wasn't going to get involved in any trouble the boss's girlfriend might be having. Going anywhere near her, even allowing himself to dream of her, was trouble with a capital *T.*

For a second he weighed what he should tell her, then decided to go with the truth. She didn't look like the type who would press someone like Mochi into child slavery. "His whole village was wiped out. His name is Mochi."

"He needs some clothes."

Jase looked over the dirty little kid in his even dirtier loincloth. Pants would have been good, at the very least. He thought of his few meager pieces of clothing, none of which would remotely fit the boy. Where was he supposed to find kid's clothing around here? Department stores didn't exactly dot the jungle.

"I can send some cloth down from the house. I'll tell Consuela to make something for him," the woman suggested.

He had a feeling Don Pedro wouldn't be pleased if he knew that his woman visited the barracks and chatted with a foot soldier. She was going to get him in trouble. But a decent chunk of cloth would have been nice. "Much appreciated."

He put a hand on Mochi's shoulder then stepped back, drawing the boy with him.

"You don't sound local."

"Part Mexican, part Zapotec, part Texan." He didn't like the way her eyes lit up at the Texan part. She better not think he would be her helping hand with her troubles. He had compromised this op badly enough already by taking responsibility for Mochi.

"I'm Melanie Key. From Austin. Do you go back to the U.S. sometimes?" She seemed to be holding her breath, waiting for the answer.

"Never." He squashed any budding hope decisively and turned Mochi around to go. "Come on, buddy."

They needed to have a talk about what areas of the compound were safe and unsafe, how to stay out of the way. This place was different than the jungle. The kid needed a whole new kind of survival training.

He nodded to Melanie and left her where she stood. He didn't know what her troubles were, but he wasn't going to get involved in them under any circumstances.

He'd learned his lesson the last time, with a Venezuelan journalist whose long legs had somehow convinced him that he had to save her from the secret police, even if that side adventure jeopardized his mission in the country. Only she'd been a counterspy, sent to turn him.

She'd been good. He'd fallen for her, and he didn't fall easily. He didn't do relationships. So sure, he had a hard time resisting damsels in distress. He enjoyed a good rescue, but at the end he always walked away.

But he wasn't going to have to walk away from Melanie, because this was one crazy side adventure he wasn't going to walk into, to start with.

He was going to have a very simple motto when it came to her and those troubled, gold-speckled eyes of hers: STAY AWAY.

DON PEDRO WAITED at the top of the stairs with a frown on his hawkish face when Melanie returned to the hacienda from the barracks. "Where have you been?"

Her heart beat in her throat as she looked up at her brother-in-law. Her body tensed. He was shorter than she, but somehow always managed to loom over her. "Stretching my legs. I needed fresh air."

"That's why you have the balcony." His small, mud-colored eyes flashed.

"Not much room here for a walk," she said good-naturedly, determined to keep things light despite the gathering tension in the air. "The men look busy. Lots of running around out there."

His thin upper lip curled. "Some idiot might be coming to challenge me. Who the hell does he think he is?" He pointed his index finger at Melanie. "You are not to leave the house. You carry my sole heir."

They never discussed it, but she sort of figured he couldn't have children of his own. And Julio, the husband she'd lost to a drunk driver in Rio seven months ago, had been Pedro's only brother.

She took the steps slowly, hoping he would move off before she reached the top, but he stayed where he stood.

He put a hand on her arm when she reached him, a milder expression replacing the anger on his face. "Come sit with me for a while. We should spend more time together." He nodded toward his bedroom.

"My back aches from the walk. I should probably lie down." She pressed her hands to the small of her back and hoped she looked drawn enough to be convincing.

Displeasure flashed in his eyes, impatience tightening the muscles of his jaw. He watched her closely, as if contemplating whether or not to push, but at the end he let her go. "We wouldn't want to harm the child."

He wanted her son first and foremost. He wanted her, too, in his bed, although not nearly as badly. But once he had her baby...

"You'll stay inside," he said, his voice hard steel again, before he turned to stalk into his office.

When he'd been at the family mansion in the city, he'd consorted with models and actresses. She'd seen the type of women; she'd attended a number of his lavish receptions. There, he acted the successful businessman, all charm and generosity. Here in camp, where he at last showed his true face, the cooking women served his basic needs. She'd heard the noises, would no doubt hear them again today when one of them brought Pedro's lunch up to him.

She hurried to her room and locked the door behind her before he could decide he wanted to deviate from the routine. She sank into the chair in the corner and put her feet on the small stool. Her ankles were swelling again.

Her baby kicked. She pressed her hand against the spot, loving the feel of that connection. Part of her couldn't wait to see her son, part of her panicked at the thought that in a month, he would be born and she would become a mother.

She wasn't ready.

She'd planned on growing up before the baby came. She'd wanted and needed to change. She needed to become a strong and independent woman, because that was the sort of mother she wanted to be. She had planned on doing a lot of work on herself before they got to this stage.

Then Pedro had trapped her and derailed her plans. Nothing was going to happen now as she'd planned it. She thought of the pretty nursery she'd been working on in her apartment back in Rio. The crib. That was where she'd planned to raise her baby, not here.

She pushed to her feet and waddled over to the armoire, bent—not without some difficulty—and fished out the backpack she'd come here with. The bag was on the smallish side, but she wasn't going on a long trip. And she couldn't carry too much extra weight anyway. She was carrying enough already.

She put the bag on the bed and closed her eyes for a second. God, she really *was* going to do this.

She'd been in denial these past few months. She hadn't believed Pedro was really going to hold her here. She'd thought he would come to his senses, reach deep and find some last, forgotten shred of decency.

He hadn't. She'd made a mistake to think that because he was Julio's brother, the two men would be similar in some basic way. But Pedro wasn't bound by any sense of honor. Pedro did what he wanted, took what he wanted.

She knew that now, but it was almost too late.

She packed some clothes—a pair of lightweight maternity pants and a long-sleeved shirt—most of the fruit from the fruit bowl on the table, her box of prenatal vitamins and the antimalaria pills she'd been taking faithfully.

She could hear Pedro talking to someone at the top of the landing. She listened for the voices, trying to gauge whether they were coming closer. Locked door or not, if he knocked, she would have to let him in. Otherwise, he'd just kick the door in. He'd done that before.

She hurried.

Jase. She tasted the name on her lips. He was the one. He was going to save her.

Trouble was coming. She'd caught the sense of increased tension, caught bits and pieces of talk here and there, saw the hustle and bustle outside. She wanted to be gone by the time the fighting began. Or before her sinister brother-in-law completely lost his patience with her.

Jase seemed to be different than the average thug around camp. That he was part American had to count for something. And while he looked just as hard-edged and dangerous as the others, he didn't have that sense of depravity about him that defined the rest of Pedro's men.

Plus, he was attracted to her on some level. That had been apparent in his graphite-gray eyes before he shuttered them. She'd stifled the answering twinge of awareness. Well, of course, she would notice those eyes and that body. Those hard muscles— Were something she was *not* going to think about. She refused to be attracted to anyone who would work for a man like her brother-in-law.

She'd sworn off men, anyway, especially the alpha male type. Her father had controlled her long enough. Julio had seemed nice, but had quickly turned all macho, head of the house, you'll-do-as-told, after the wedding. And Don Pedro...

She shuddered when she thought of what her life would become if she couldn't get away from here.

She put a few extra items into the bag, then looked into the rustic mirror on the wall. "If you don't want others to control your life, then don't let them," she said the words out loud, voicing the resolution she'd come to while she'd tossed and turned through all those sleepless nights in the jungle's humid heat.

There was only one solution: *she* had to take control.

She had to get herself out of here. And she would, using Jase somehow to achieve her goal. He was the key to her escape. And she would do whatever it took to get away from here. She'd been praying for a rescuer for too long—a police raid, or drug bust, anything. But nobody was coming. She had to accept at last that saving herself would be up to her. She fisted her hands. She *would* get away from this cursed place. And once she did, no man was ever going to control her life again.

"Some years from now, we're going to meet a nice, mellow guy who loves kids," she promised her baby. "Maybe a low-key music teacher," she added. She liked music.

But first she would have to deal with Jase.

She stashed the backpack under her bed. Step one, completed.

Now on to step two. Somehow, she had to trick Jase into helping her. She couldn't blackmail or threaten him into it. She had a feeling he wouldn't find her overly threatening. That left bribery. In exchange for his assistance, she would give him something he wanted. And since she had no money, the only avenue left to her was seduction.

The thought of what that might entail filled her with mixed emotions. But she drew a deep breath and strengthened her resolve. She placed a hand on her abdomen. "I'm going to do whatever it takes to get us out of here." She would go to any length to save her baby.

THE MEN SPENT the morning preparing for battle. No teams had left the camp on their scheduled transport trips. Runners were sent to the teams who were out with orders to return to the camp posthaste. The downstairs of the main house brimmed with the Don's closest men. Everyone expected the fighting to begin by the following morning.

Cristobal's men were still some hours away, and they wouldn't want to fight as soon as they got here. They would want to map the terrain first, get a good night's sleep.

Jase had been turned away at the door when he'd gone up to the hacienda to discuss taking over Paulo's position in packing. Roberto had other priorities right now. He was focused on strengthening the camp's defenses and didn't have time for ambitious foot soldiers.

So Jase dropped that plan and had gone back an hour later, pretending to be looking for Lucas. He'd gotten turned away once again. By noon, he was still no closer to planting the bug, and his nerves hummed with frustration.

He hated the waiting part of undercover ops. Of course, 90 percent of undercover ops consisted of waiting. He'd made progress over the past couple of months, had gained important information, but he wanted to have that damn bug planted already.

He walked by the main house every chance he got. On his fifth pass, he spotted Melanie on the balcony once again. He would have been lying if he said he didn't feel a little thrill when her eyes settled on him.

"You," she said in a bossy tone. "Come right up. I need you to help me move something."

Exactly the break he needed. He stifled a grin and put on an expression of mindless obedience. "*Sí, señora.* Right away."

Having heard the exchange, the man at the door let him through at last. Half a dozen men stood around the table in the large room he walked into, a combination foyer-slash-living-room area that had been converted into a war room.

The men glanced up at his entrance, but nobody questioned him. They trusted the guard at the door not to let in anyone who didn't have any business being in there. They were all busy drawing up battle plans and arguing with each other.

Jase headed straight for the stairs.

That did draw attention.

"Hey," Roberto called after him. "Where do you think you're going?"

He hunched his shoulders, put his head down, making himself into the very picture of subservience. "The *señora* wants me to move some furniture."

Roberto rolled his eyes, probably thinking how it was just like a woman to be interior decorating with an impending battle looming over their heads. Which was exactly what Jase was thinking, so he shot an I-know-what-you-mean look back at the man and shook his head slightly.

Roberto waved him on with a disgusted gesture and returned to his battle planning.

No need to hurry now. Jase noted every door, every hallway, every man. He planned on getting a good look around upstairs as well, but as he reached the top of the stairs, he found the woman waiting for him in her open doorway.

She wore white this time, a linen dress designed for the climate and to accommodate her motherly curves.

"In here." She gestured with impatience. "I need this couch moved out of the sun. I want it in the far corner." She drew into the middle of the room.

He followed her. Did she know that a battle was coming? Did she trust Don Pedro so blindly that she didn't realize how much danger she was in? Cristobal would be no pushover. He'd all but obliterated the Don's previous headquarters. The man was playing to win.

"I just want to be more comfortable," she was saying.

Silk pillows, fans, a sprawling bed with mosquito netting, books and stacks of magazines filled the large space. The Don had clearly settled her in for a long stay. She could have run a small convenience store out of her room.

He tried not to think of the stark contrast between the barracks and her room, between what she had at her disposal and what Mochi had, sleeping on the floor next to the stove in the kitchen. She was the boss's pampered girlfriend. She lived in a different world from the rest of them. That bothered him, but he didn't let it show.

He grabbed the end of the couch and dragged the damned thing to where she pointed. Took him about three seconds. But she didn't look pleased. She looked disappointed.

"Wrong spot?"

She shook her head, looking at him with something akin to panic. Which made him wonder just what was going on in that beautiful head of hers. Then the next second, her whole demeanor changed, as if she'd just thought of something.

"Thank you." Her full lips stretched into a smile. "Would you like a glass of cold tea?"

Definitely. Especially if she kept smiling at him like that. But that quick change in her demeanor made him uneasy. "I better get going."

"It's just—" She looked away. "It'd be great to talk to another American. I get lonely up here."

The bossy attitude she'd displayed on the balcony was gone. Maybe she only used that tone around the men to assure their respect and to make sure they wouldn't perceive her as weak. But she seemed to be letting her guard down around him. Whatever the reason, her vulnerability grabbed him as nothing else could have, and somewhat mollified him. She did look lonely, and desperate, suddenly, in some way.

"I can't imagine Don Pedro would neglect a woman as beautiful as you are," he told her in a light tone, still feeling that more was going on here than what was being said.

But instead of lightening the mood, his words made her frown.

"I'm not his…" She actually blushed.

He couldn't remember the last time he saw a woman do that. Certainly didn't expect it from a drug lord's live-in girlfriend. Interesting.

"I was married to his brother," she told him.

Huh. And the plot thickens.

He'd damn near memorized the Don's file while preparing for this op. The man had a brother, Julio, in Brazil, who'd been killed a few months back in a car accident. Jase didn't remember any mention of a wife.

Did her existence and presence here change anything? Was this something he could use to his advantage? More specifically: was she a threat to his mission or an opportunity?

"Do you like it here?" he asked noncommittally. Better tread softly until he figured her out.

The abject misery that crossed her face couldn't be faked. Her slim shoulders sagged. "I wish I could go home."

"Why don't you?"

"Don Pedro prefers to keep me safe, close to him."

Now that was a carefully worded sentence if he'd ever heard one. Could or could not mean that the Don was holding her against her will.

He didn't have to think long to find a reason why that might happen. Since the Don's family had been ravaged in years of drug wars, her child would be the man's closest living family. In a patriarchal society, that meant everything. The Don would take the relation more than seriously.

"You've known him long?" Jase asked her, still not fully understanding why she would ever come to a jungle camp like this in the first place, especially in her condition.

She sank onto the couch, graceful despite the extra weight she carried. "I met Julio, my husband, in Rio. He saved me one night when my car broke down in a bad neighborhood. We were married before I knew it. Then three weeks later he was killed in a car accident."

"What were you doing in Rio?"

"Finishing my master's on sustainable high-density housing in developing nations."

The slum recovery projects. He'd heard of those. Building them gave people jobs, then when the buildings were done, it got them off the streets. "Don Pedro was there?" That he couldn't picture for anything, not unless he'd been recruiting runners for his drug trade, but at his level in the organization, he wouldn't do that personally.

She shook her head. "When Julio died, I called the number he had for his family. Don Pedro asked me to bring Julio's ashes to Bogota for a family funeral. That's when I met Pedro. I was a guest at the family mansion in the city for a while. Then he brought me here." She winced. "I didn't exactly understand what this place was. He told me we were going to his house in the country."

The tone of her voice said she hadn't been given much choice about coming. So maybe she *was* being held here against her will. He didn't like the way that thought brought out his protective instincts.

As far as he knew, Julio had been a two-bit restaurant owner in Rio. He'd gone there in his early twenties to get away from the family business. Meeting the Don must have been a pretty big shock for his widow, if he hadn't told her anything about his brother—which seemed to be the case.

He watched her with renewed interest, trying to figure out whether she was the snooty *señora* who'd ordered him around just minutes ago, or a woman out of her depth, in serious trouble.

Her shoulders straightened under his scrutiny, and a smile came onto her face that looked more forced than real.

"Why don't you sit?" She motioned to the spot on the couch next to her.

Suspicion pricked his instincts. Until now, he stood in line with the open door, visible from the outside for propriety's sake. He'd assumed she would want that.

Maybe he was mistaken. He sat next to her, still leaving a respectable amount of space between them, curious where this all might lead. He was almost sure now that she was plotting something and calling him up to move the couch had only been a ploy. She clearly wanted something from him, but wasn't sure how to go about it.

She bit her full bottom lip. And put her hand on his knee.

He nearly jumped right off the couch as heat shot up his leg.

Okay, he hadn't expected *that*.

If he were a gentleman, he would have stopped her

right there, would have told her to come right out with it and tell him what she wanted from him. But he'd been too long without female companionship, so he stayed where he was and put an expectant smile on his face.

He waited to see her next move. At the very least, it should prove to be interesting.

She pulled her hand back and cleared her throat. He could almost see the wheels turning in her head. She was trying to figure out how to go about getting him to do whatever it was that she wanted from him.

A seductress she was not, which made the situation even more intriguing. And turned him on completely. He leaned back, watching and waiting. Leaving his knee within easy reach.

A man could hope.

She gave him another tremulous smile as the air between them filled with tension. Her gaze dropped to his mouth, and she licked her lips in a nervous gesture.

Which brought his X-rated dreams about her to mind. Was she thinking about kissing him?

The temperature in the room shot up a couple of degrees. She had the most kissable mouth he'd ever seen, with a slight crease in the middle of the bottom lip. And all of a sudden he couldn't take his eyes off her full lips.

She leaned a little closer.

He couldn't believe it.

She looked so nervous it was a toss-up whether she'd kiss him or run away first.

Every cell in his body voted for the first option. He held very still, careful not to scare her away.

She leaned another inch closer. And looked pitifully miserable about it, while trying to keep a come-hither smile on her face. Not very convincing. He had half a

mind to close the distance between them just to put her
out of her misery.

The more she fidgeted, the better the idea seemed.
For some reason, he was desperate all of a sudden to
feel those full lips pressed against his. She smelled like
flowers, which made him wonder what she would taste
like. He was betting on honey.

In the end, he wasn't sure who made the last small
move that brought them together.

Her soft lips tasted like sweet papaya. Okay, that was
more logical and likely than honey. They had papaya
on the menu pretty much every single day. Good thing
he really liked it.

An odd, exhilarating feeling hit him like a lightning
bolt out of nowhere and sent his head spinning. He
wanted to sink into her sweetness, to take her up—here
and now—on everything she was reluctantly offering.

Dozens of erotic images filled his mind, ridiculously
hot compared to how chaste the kiss was. He wanted to
lay her down on that couch, wanted to bare her breasts
to his gaze and mouth. He wanted to see her eyes cloud-
ing with pleasure.

He pressed closer and licked the corner of her lips.
She gave a soft, startled sigh, but didn't move back.
If anything, she leaned toward him. Hot need plowed
through him like a freight train.

He wanted her naked.

He put his hands over her rib cage, his fingers spread
out, his thumbs massaging the spot under her breasts.
Considering her earlier display of nerves, he expected
her to protest.

She didn't.

In the back of his mind, he was aware of the open

door. He knew if someone walked by, it would mean instant execution. They'd drag him outside and shoot him like a dog. He *was* a dog, for taking advantage of her like this.

Yet with Melanie's lips on his, the guilt and the risk didn't seem so grave, and was certainly worth it.

He knew he was in trouble when he realized he was thinking like a hormone-crazed teenage boy and not like a trained operative. Still, everything he was pushed him to proceed with the seduction.

Only the sure knowledge that she was playing him could make him pull away.

She looked shocked and disconcerted, her eyes wide with disbelief. Not because he'd pulled back, he suspected, but because she'd done what she had. She was probably surprised that she'd actually gone through with it.

So was he.

He watched as that hesitant smile returned to her lips. He had to give her credit for pulling herself together in short order.

"Perhaps we could go someplace more private," she suggested, and swallowed hard.

His body sang with pleasure at the suggestion, even if he couldn't follow through with it under any circumstances. "Such as?" he asked anyway.

"Down by the river?"

Again, images from his dream came back to him. But so did her whispered prayer from the night before, a clear image as she had stood up there on the balcony. And it put things into perspective.

He was to be her ticket out of the compound.

She glanced away, and he followed her gaze. A

backpack peeked from under the bed, no doubt holding her escape kit. Did she have a weapon? Guns were all around the place, always handy. Getting her hands on one shouldn't have been too difficult.

Did she plan on shooting him once he got her far enough from this place? She looked all soft on the outside, but a glint in her eyes told him that she had found a steel core somewhere deep down, a core he'd do better not to trifle with.

But how he wanted to. Trifle with her. Preferably while they were both naked.

"I don't think that's a good idea." There. He still had some common sense left, and his response to her proved it.

He took another look at her lips. Then he stood and walked away from her before he could do something colossally stupid, like kiss her again.

Chapter Three

Jase strode to the stairs without looking back. Who knew that with all the cold-blooded killers inside the hacienda, Melanie's room would be the most dangerous part of the house? He wasn't scared of the men. He'd been well trained to take care of thugs like Don Pedro's. With Melanie, on the other hand, for the first time in his life, he felt out of his depth.

He didn't like the feeling.

She'd somehow managed to turn him on while, at the same time, massively confusing him.

The only thing weirder than her hitting on him was his instant attraction to her. That'd come out of nowhere. He didn't have a pregnant woman fetish or anything. Never had a pregnant girlfriend. Wasn't even sure if pregnant women were into men or were awash with some mommy hormones that preoccupied them, making things like sex irrelevant. Those labor and delivery scenes he'd seen in movies flashed into his mind, scenes where the woman screamed at the father and did her best to break the man's fingers.

He flexed his hands.

He hadn't planned on doing that. Ever.

Yet he found Melanie sexy as hell. And enigmatic.

With a touch of vulnerability. But with enough guts to go after what she wanted.

Okay. Boyish obsession ends now.

He shuffled down the stairs, his neck tucked in, doing his best not to draw attention to himself, noting the two men who'd come in since he'd gone upstairs. If nobody paid attention to him, maybe he could hang around a few more minutes.

He glanced around, looking for one of the Don's satellite phones, but he didn't see any of them out in plain sight. Bugging that would be just as effective as bugging the man's office, and possibly easier to accomplish.

A faint taste of Melanie still lingered on his lips, reminding him that months had passed since he'd last touched a woman. Melanie had reawakened his body and then some, but only danger awaited him in that direction, so he refocused his thoughts on the men by the table. They were eating, holding bowls of steaming food the women must have brought up while Jase had been upstairs.

His stomach growled. He ignored it.

Roberto, who wasn't eating, spotted him and called out as he wrestled with a sizable roll of paper. "Come give me a hand. Here. Hold this."

Okay. Good. Excellent, in fact.

A command to stay instead of a lecture on all the reasons he shouldn't be in here.

The man struggled to spread out a large jungle map on a table, a taped-together puzzle of what looked like Google Maps printouts.

Jase moved to hold down two corners, spotted the satellite phone under the edge of the paper. Roberto grabbed a hand grenade to weigh down another corner, then pulled his knife and speared the last corner to the wood with the blade. He gave a swarthy grin, apparently satisfied with his own ingenuity.

"Let's see if we can figure this out, amigos." He bent to carefully examine the expanse of trees, interrupted here and there by the river or a clearing. He pointed to the middle of the map and followed the line of the river to the point where it looped back on itself a little. "We're here."

None of the camp showed. The satellite pictures had probably been taken years ago, when the camp had been nothing but a couple of wood huts hidden under the trees. Only after Don Pedro's headquarters had been destroyed by Cristobal last year had the boss begun serious building here.

The men examined the map as they ate.

"Here is one of the burned villages." One of them pointed at the edge of the map with his fork.

"And here is another." Roberto tapped a spot not far from the first. "So we know Cristobal is going to hit us from the southeast."

Jase scanned the map in every direction. He hadn't seen a rendering this detailed of the area before. He'd studied aerial photos of the jungle before leaving on this mission, but back then he hadn't yet known where exactly the Don's new headquarters were, so he'd had no reason to inspect this exact spot out of the endless jungle specifically.

Some sort of a building showed on the satellite map about thirty miles to the north of them.

"What's that?" he asked, not sure whether he would get an answer.

But Roberto seemed to be in a talkative mood. "A

scientific research station. They monitor one square mile of jungle and record every animal that passes through it. Some kind of biodiversity research. A chopper brings them supplies and switches staff out every month. They don't move outside their boundaries."

"They got any good stuff?" Jase played the part of the opportunistic jungle thug, wondering if the scientists knew just how close they were to some serious trouble.

Roberto shrugged. "Not the kind of equipment we could use here. And their perimeter security is too good. That's how they keep track of the animals. They're not worth the bother."

Jase filed that information away in his brain and kept his mouth shut while the others marked the approximate location of the enemy troops on the map and tried to guess the numbers. He paid close attention until a shout from above interrupted the murmur of voices.

"What the hell are you doing? In your room!" Don Pedro growled at Melanie at the top of the stairs, his eyes narrowed with fury, his mouth drawn into a sharp, cruel line of displeasure.

Looked like the Don had stepped out of his office and caught her watching the men from above. No doubt she'd been plotting her escape, picking the next chump to try her tricks on.

If the Don had come out earlier when Jase'd been in her room…

He thanked his lucky stars and watched as she headed toward her door, her neck pulled in. Apparently she didn't move quickly enough. The Don grabbed her by the arm. Hard enough to leave marks.

Jase's muscles tightened.

Her hands slid in a protective gesture to her abdomen as she tried to pull away. She winced as the man shoved her toward her room. The door closed behind them with a slam.

Then the Don proceeded to shout at her some more in Spanish, his tirade muted now and unintelligible to the men downstairs. A small pause came, then something crashed.

Jase's muscles twitched.

She'd tried to use him and he didn't like that, but he liked this even less. Instinct, and everything he was, pushed him to leap up the stairs and bust into that room. But his training held him back, even as his jaw muscles pulled tighter with every passing second.

Keep it cool. Don't break cover.

The Don was obviously having a bad day. Having his mortal enemy, Cristobal, who'd nearly brought him down not that long ago, marching on his camp had visibly rattled the big boss. Jase had never seen him look anything less than invincible before.

He'd rather see him dead, all considered.

He noted the position of every man in the room again, each weapon, calculated angles and speed, shifted into a better position without letting go of the map. If she cried out…

But even as he thought that, the Don stormed out of Melanie's room and yelled down below for everyone to work before disappearing in his office once again. The men shrugged off the display of temper—nothing they hadn't seen before. None of them seemed to care one whit for the woman upstairs. They were all focused on the upcoming battle.

The bastard had slammed Melanie's door so hard behind him that it'd bounced open again. Jase kept watching that gap in the door from the corner of his eye while he pretended to pay attention to Roberto and the others.

Then he caught movement. The door closed with a quiet click.

She was all right then—well enough, at least, to get up and move around. He relaxed marginally. Of course, the Don wouldn't risk hurting the baby.

But after the baby was born... Jase rolled the tension out of his shoulders. Okay, so maybe she had a good reason for wanting to get away from this place, sooner rather than later.

She either ran now, or she would have to take her chances here.

Pretty soon she'd be too far along in the pregnancy to risk a trek through the jungle. And she couldn't run once the baby was born. A newborn wouldn't survive the grueling trek. Plus, once the baby was born, the Don would no longer need her. Who knew how long after the birth the Don would let her live. Any of the camp women could be brought up to the house to take care of the kid.

Jase didn't blame her for trying to use him to gain her freedom. A part of him even wished he could help. He was drawn to Melanie in a way he hadn't been drawn to any of the others.

But more than her life was at stake here.

By bringing down the Don, he would be saving thousands eventually.

He pushed thoughts of the woman aside. His full attention needed to be on the men. He had to be vigilant, to be fully present in the here and now so he wouldn't make a mistake.

"How badly do you think we're outnumbered?" one of the men wondered aloud.

Roberto shot him a glare.

Some of these men had been present at the fight at the previous camp and knew Cristobal was no pushover. Their losses in that fight had been rough.

Jase kept his eyes hooded, pretending to be studying the map, but studied the men one by one instead. Could he find an ally among them, somebody who would be willing to provide information? Would any consider defection?

If they had any reservations about the boss upstairs, they kept quiet about it. None would dare to air any doubts in front of Roberto and risk looking anything but 100 percent committed.

Jase held down the corners of the map and considered the satellite phone that made a bump under the paper. The phone was big and clumsy compared to his super spy phone that he'd lost crossing a mangrove swamp with Lucas and the others a month back.

That one had been special-issue: waterproof, bulletproof to a point, even damn near fireproof. It hadn't been caiman-proof, however. When one of the large reptiles ripped away a chunk of Jase's pants, it'd swallowed the damned thing right with the fabric.

Had he been alone, he would have hunted down the toothy bastard and gutted it, but he had to let it go in the interest of preserving his cover. He couldn't go hunting for a phone nobody even knew he had.

He missed that phone, and didn't like being cut off from the men back at headquarters for the time being, but right now the Don's phone was more important. He shifted from one foot to the other, pretended that the corner of the map slipped from his hand, grabbed after the paper to roll it back out and "accidentally" knocked the phone to the floor in the process. It rolled under the table.

"Sorry, man. Didn't see that." He let the paper go and squatted to retrieve the phone, grabbing for it with his left hand while going for the bug with the right.

The cloner would duplicate the signal to a U.S. Army satellite, every future conversation would be recorded and stored on a secure server. He snapped the back off the phone with his thumb, plugged the bug in, then popped the back into place as he stood.

He put the phone back on the table, where someone else was now holding his corners of the map.

Roberto shot him an annoyed look, but he seemed too busy figuring out Cristobal's next move to pay much attention to anything else.

Jase backed away and out of the room. He cast a last look at Melanie's door, which remained firmly closed. A strange tightness appeared in the middle of his chest.

Probably heartburn. As enthusiastic as Consuela was with spices, it was a miracle he still had any stomach lining left. He rubbed the strange sensation away with the heel of his hand as he stepped out into the humid jungle air.

He strode back to the barracks, swung by the kitchen on the way. Speaking of the tequila-swigging matron... Consuela was stitching two pieces of plain linen cloth together that stood out in stark contrast against her red and orange block print muumuu. She sat on the ground, her feet extended toward Jase. She wore no shoes. She didn't need them; the inch-thick cracked and hardened layer of calluses on the bottom of her feet protected her soles just fine.

Another woman chopped sugar cane in the back. Pretty ironic. Some of the men in camp were running around like headless chickens out there, while the women went on with their chores as if the whole camp wasn't preparing for battle.

He glanced around but didn't see Mochi in any of the corners. "Where's the kid?" They'd have to have another talk about the importance of sticking around the women and keeping out of the way, especially once the fighting began.

"Alejandro came and got him," Consuela mumbled with a shrug. "His shirt is almost done."

But Jase was already turning back out the door. He hurried on toward the dog pens, broke into a run. With the camp in a complete upheaval, nobody thought his haste suspicious. Nobody stopped to question him.

The dogs perked up at the sight of him, then looked disappointed when they realized he wasn't bringing left-overs, as he often did. The animals were all scarred, but still wagging their tails, not holding an ounce of grudge toward the humans who'd chosen this life for them.

He scratched a bulky head sticking out from between the bars. The dog in the next enclosure jumped up on its hind legs, wanting attention, as well. He was almost as tall as Jase. "Hey ya, Killer." He patted that one, too, as he passed.

He'd considered, more than once, setting them free in the night. But if the wild boars and the jaguars didn't get them, they'd kill each other. As much as he hated to see them taken to the towns to be abused in the ring, he couldn't come up with a decent plan to save them.

They'd be in his report when he finally got out of here. Their best hope was a U.S. military hit on the camp. They would be liberated then.

He didn't get all the way past the enclosures when Jorge, round as a rain barrel, shuffled from the back, smoking a fat cigar and cleaning his weapon. He gave a yellow-toothed grin in anticipation of the battle.

"Have you seen Alejandro?" Jase peered behind him.

"He was here with the kid." Jorge shook his head, a look of annoyance flashing across his weather-beaten face. "Took Chico."

Chico was a three-legged puppy, injured by one of the older dogs. Since he obviously wasn't going to grow up to be a great fighter, he didn't have much of a future at the camp. A miracle that nobody had shot him yet.

"Alejandro took Chico?" That didn't make much sense. Alejandro wasn't exactly the type to adopt a handicapped puppy.

Jorge took the cigar out of his mouth and spat on the ground. "I gave Chico to the kid. Couldn't stand all that caterwauling. Alejandro's damn fault. He wanted the boy to take his two best dogs into the jungle to make sure they don't get hurt in the shooting. Idiot. One dog, the kid could handle. But when Alejandro gave the boy the second leash, the two dogs fought like crazy."

Of course they would. They were trained to fight each other. What the hell did the idiot expect? Jase didn't have to be psychic to know how that turned out. Fury swept through him. "Where are they?"

"Up in packaging."

He cut across the compound, breaking into a run once again.

Roberto stepped outside from the hacienda as Jase passed by.

"Everybody needs to get ready before nightfall. I want everyone to get some sleep before the battle starts in the morning. Make sure you have your weapons together and enough ammo. And no drinking tonight."

Jase acknowledged the orders with a nod, but didn't stop to talk.

He found the packaging building in chaos, holes dug in the floor, tightly wrapped bricks of cocaine being buried in every corner. The men resented the extra work, swearing deliberately, cursing Cristobal.

Jase ignored them. "Mochi?"

Someone nodded toward the west wall. Jase zigzagged through between the sweating men, careful not to knock anyone over. Tempers were running high. He didn't have time to stop for a fistfight.

Mochi sat on the floor, his arm bleeding, shiny tear tracks marking his face that lit up with hope when he spotted Jase. He held a wiggling flour sack under one arm. Chico, presumably.

Alejandro was holding out his finger to the boy, with a dash of white powder on the tip. He, too, glanced up as Jase reached them.

"For the pain." His expression was challenging and defensive at the same time, as if he hadn't decided yet which one to go with.

As much as he hated Jase's claim on the boy, he knew he had to respect it according to camp rules. He knew he'd done wrong damaging the kid. He knew Jase could call him out over that and demand compensation, maybe even the knife back. All that flashed through his gaze.

Jase knocked his hand away with a growl, holding

back from doing more, then grabbed Mochi's hand and pulled him up. "Come on, buddy. Consuela will take care of you. Let's get you out of here."

Mochi scrambled to bring his sack.

"Just because he's yours, it don't mean he don't have to work off his keep," Alejandro called after them, his voice belligerent, showing off for the others. "If the camp needs help, he still needs to pitch in."

Jase turned back, his temper hanging by a thread. He flashed a hard glare at the bastard. "He's not going to be any use to the Don if you kill him."

The mention of the boss subdued Alejandro somewhat, but didn't wipe nearly enough hate off his face. He might have acknowledged Jase's claim on the boy, but he didn't like it.

They would probably have to fight that fight someday to settle it once and for all. But not today. An open confrontation with the man at this moment would solve nothing and would endanger the op. And they all had better things to do the day before the battle.

"Let me see the wound," Jase told Mochi as they moved on.

The kid lifted his scrawny arm carefully.

Jase swore under his breath at the bleeding, ragged gash where sharp canine teeth had ripped the skin. Probably by accident. The kid had gotten trapped between two fighting dogs. The dogs were doing what they'd been trained to do. Wasn't their fault.

The blame lay with him. He'd brought the boy here.

And he hadn't been able to watch the kid as closely as he would have liked. That had to change. He couldn't keep the kid next to him 24/7. Sooner or later, something bad would happen to Mochi here. The camp was

dangerous enough and now, with Cristobal coming…
It was no place for a kid.

Or a pregnant woman, the voice of conscience said
in his head. *Forget about her,* the voice of reason coun-
tered.

Getting Mochi away would be difficult enough, and
his disappearance would bother few people. They all
had bigger things to worry about. But if Melanie went
missing with the Don's heir, the man would search
heaven and earth to find her.

"You'll be fine. Consuela will give you good medicine," Jase reassured the boy, hoping he understood at
least the gist of his words.

So far he'd barely spoken, but he seemed to follow
direction for the most part, so he must know at least
a little Spanish. His village had probably had enough
contact with loggers and the Don's men for him to pick
up a couple of words here and there.

They passed by the hacienda. Jase glanced up at the
empty balcony. Then he rolled his shoulders to get rid
of that tight feeling that came into his chest once again.

He couldn't save everyone. He would do the best he
could, and live with the consequences.

Mochi wiped his face, then opened the mouth of the
bag and lifted it, proudly showing off the fur ball inside.

"Yeah, just what we needed," Jase groused, looking into those puppy eyes, determined not to get taken
in by them.

Mochi snuggled the bag back into the crook of his
arm, then took Jase's hand again, his little fingers tightening around his.

He looked at the boy who'd placed all his innocent

trust in him, unconditionally, then thought of the research station to the north.

He hadn't planned on going there. He hadn't planned on going anywhere until he had the information he'd come for: names, dates, locations.

But the station was Mochi's best chance.

And if he was going to try to save the kid, tonight had to be the night. He strode forward, trying to organize a couple of disjointed thoughts into something that might resemble a workable plan.

Maybe he wouldn't have to go all the way to the research station. He might meet a hunting party from one of the villages and turn the kid over to them. At least then the kid would be with his own people. Either way, step one was to get the kid out of the camp.

He'd have to sneak Mochi out somehow. And Mochi only. The puppy had to stay. It would whine at inopportune moments and pee all over the place, drawing predators to them as they walked through the jungle. They would have to move fast and without being detected. They couldn't afford any handicaps. Which was why he couldn't drag along a pregnant woman either.

Melanie would have to take her chances with the rest of them in camp. Since she carried the Don's heir, the man would protect her with the lives of all of his men, if needed.

The puppy would have to stay with Consuela. He didn't want to take him back to the dog pens where the men would get rid of him the first time he got underfoot. The kitchen had a rat problem. Maybe the puppy could be trained to deal with it.

Jase reached into his pocket, counted the pesos he

had left. He had more than enough to convince the woman to take good care of one little puppy.

If only all his problems could be solved that easily.

The perimeter was as tightly guarded as it had ever been, every eye open, watching for Cristobal's men. Would have been great if Jase was one of the dozen guys on guard duty tonight, but he wasn't. Alejandro was, however. Unfortunately, the man was unlikely to do him any favors.

"Are you hungry?" he asked the boy as they neared the kitchen.

Consuela flew toward them from the doorway, looking at the kid's bloody arm. *"Ay, Dios mio!"* She picked up Mochi, swearing like a sailor at Jase for bringing the boy back in this shape.

He ignored her accusing glare. "Do you have anything for the wound?"

"Sí, sí." The woman shooed him away.

He had a fair idea what the treatment would be. Astringent plant juices, then leaf-cutter ants to close the skin. They had incredibly strong mandibles and were nature's sutures around here. The natives held them up to the wound until they grabbed on to it on each side, then twisted the body off, leaving the head and mandibles in place, which held tight long after the ant's death.

"I'll be back in a little while. I need to talk to you." he told the woman.

Then he patted the boy's head. "You hang tough, buddy. I'm going to take care of you, all right?"

He left them and headed back to the barracks, putting a plan together. If he was going to save anyone, he needed to start getting ready right now. They had no time to waste.

Chapter Four

Dusk gathered outside, the day nearly over. Time was passing way too fast. Melanie stood by her desk, madly digging through the drawer, picking up and discarding items from the clutter, looking for something skinny, something that was stiff but also bendable. Nothing. She slammed the drawer shut, then stared at the old Spanish dueling pistol Pedro had given her to shoot herself with if she thought she would be taken by Cristobal's men.

Seriously.

She sank into the chair behind her. How on earth had she ended up here, at this point in her life? Her hand shook as she lifted the weapon. *This is what you get when you let other people make your choices.*

But never again—if she survived this. Never again.

She turned the gun. Looked straight into the barrel. She'd received one bullet only, in the chamber. Her brother-in-law didn't trust her with more. He hadn't made it to where he was by being stupid.

She lowered the weapon and turned to look out the window, into the settling dusk. A dozen men were hustling along out there, preparing for the upcoming battle. Jase wasn't among them.

Wouldn't have mattered if she did spot him at this

point. She was locked into her room. She'd waited too long.

Another mistake.

She felt heavy and tired, her brain hormone-flooded. She wasn't exactly operating on all cylinders, just enough to see all her mistakes clearly. Whoever had said hindsight was twenty-twenty hadn't been kidding.

She should have run away right at the beginning, when she'd first gotten here. She'd been a lot more nimble on her feet back then, probably could have made it—if not out of the jungle, at least to the nearest settlement. From having overheard the men talking over the past months, she knew there were a handful of small villages not far from here and a research station to the north, plus a Jesuit mission.

But back then, she'd still believed that the Don would take her back to the city eventually. Months had passed by the time she'd finally realized that he had no intention of doing that, despite his promises. Then she'd wasted more time looking for an ally, examining each man who had access to the hacienda, and discarding each possibility.

She'd found Jase too late.

She had failed.

A sense of defeat washed over her.

Then her baby kicked.

"Okay, okay. I'm not giving up. Give me a second to wallow, then I'll think of something." She couldn't fold. She owed her son better than that.

"I'm going to get us out of here," she promised. Then panic bubbled up her throat as she pushed the gun away. Could she really make it to safety? What if—

The baby kicked again.

"I hear you." She steeled herself. She *was* going to escape. Or die trying. She wasn't going to sit around until things got so bad that the only way out would be to shoot herself.

Okay then. First things first.

She needed to set aside the problem of the door for a minute, and do something she *was* capable of doing.

She dressed, keeping the night in mind, putting on dark maternity slacks and a dark top, a lightweight dark shirt on top of that, a dark blue scarf wrapped around her neck. She slipped her swollen feet into her single pair of hiking boots, could barely bend low enough to tie the laces.

Tugging on the shirt must have loosened the barrette in her hair, because it slipped to the floor when she bent to her boots. She stared at it for a moment, then grinned.

She broke the barrette apart to make a slim metal strip. She tried to manipulate the lock with that. Minutes clicked by as she twisted the small tool this way and that, but achieved nothing.

She straightened too quickly, pushed by frustration, and upset the tray on the small table by the door. Her leftover lunch, which Consuela had forgotten to retrieve, dumped at her feet. The fork! Why hadn't she thought of that before? She rushed to grab it, then bent the prongs to a shape she thought would work best. Adjusted the angle after the first try. Still no luck.

Tears of frustration gathered in her eyes. She dropped the fork, wiped away the tears and waddled back to the table for the gun. She could shoot the lock. Maybe. She'd never shot a gun before. She had no idea if she could hit a target that small.

One bullet. Her hand shook. *Oh, God. Sure. No pressure.*

Then another thought occurred to her. Even if she did manage to destroy the lock, she had no idea how many people were downstairs and would come running. Stealth had to be a big part of her getaway plan. If she didn't have that, she didn't have much of anything.

She lowered the gun.

Then she raised it again. Maybe by some miracle the house was empty. Maybe by the time the men outside figured out where the shot had come from, she could escape through the hacienda's back door.

She aimed the weapon. Then jumped when an explosion shook the air. It had come from the back of the camp.

Her heart raced. Could the enemy already be here?

She rushed to the window and watched the men run off in the direction of the explosion. Half a dozen of them ran out the hacienda's front door to follow the others.

Good. Maybe they were all gone now. Hope took flight in her chest. She could do this. If the enemy was here, so much the better. Maybe in the confusion she could get away unseen.

Her baby deserved better than this.

Maybe she should have been more careful about marrying Julio. Maybe she should have researched her husband's family more thoroughly before agreeing to bring his ashes to the family crypt. Maybe she was a foolish woman, blinded by sentimental notions of love, and she deserved what she got, but her baby was innocent.

"Dear Lord, please help us get away from here." She whispered the words heavenward and aimed the gun once again, just as the door banged open, about giving her a heart attack.

Jase stood in the doorway, his wide shoulders nearly filling it. His graphite-gray eyes were fierce, his gaze unflinching as he took her in.

Her knees shook with fright.

Shoot! Self-preservation screamed in her head. But her fingers seemed frozen on the trigger.

Did he come on the Don's orders to guard her during the battle? Or did he come on his own, in the hopes of finishing what they'd started the last time he'd been up here?

"You should never hold a gun on a man unless you're planning on killing him." He strode in, annoyance all over his face. He pushed her weapon aside. "I'll get you out of here. But just so you know, I don't like it." He grabbed her backpack from under the bed. "You will do exactly what I tell you, every step of the way. Is that clear?"

How did he know where she kept her runaway emergency bag? She stood frozen to the spot for a second, too stunned to move, trying to process everything. Her chance to get away from Pedro had come at last, but only by having another man take control of her. That had never led to anything but disaster in the past.

He shot her an impatient look. "Are you coming?"

She held on to her pistol as she rushed out the door after him. She wasn't giving into his power, she told herself. She was just using him to get her out of here.

For once, not a single one of Pedro's men hung out downstairs. She followed Jase out the back. He seemed to be taking the exact route she had planned.

The boy, Mochi, waited for him outside the door.

Okay, she hadn't expected that. The kid held a flour sack that seemed to be moving. Must have been a trick of the descending darkness, or a figment of her jumpy nerves.

Jase picked up the large camouflage backpack that sat at the boy's feet and swung it over his shoulders, carrying hers in his left hand, leaving the right free for his weapon.

"If you want to live, keep up the pace," he told them, then began running toward the perimeter fence.

Once they were close he ordered them to stay in the cover of a ramshackle shed, one of the originals that the humid air and the vegetation had slowly eaten apart over the years.

He dropped the backpacks and strode toward the fence. He called out, "Jorge? What the hell is this?"

The man guarding the section came running. Melanie pulled back into the deep shadows, drawing Mochi with her, holding her breath. The little boy snuggled up to her. The flour sack wiggled against her leg. Okay, the boy definitely had something in there. But now was not the time to ask questions.

"Qué pasa?" The man stopped next to Jase, peering into the jungle, his rifle pointed at the dark forest.

"Someone cut the fence." Jase gestured, bringing the man's attention closer.

When Jorge bent to investigate the breach, Jase grabbed him from behind and in one violent motion broke his neck, then dropped him to the soft pile of leaves that covered the ground.

Melanie's stomach rolled. She was going to be sick.

But then she gritted her teeth. *No,* she wasn't. She was taking control. She was running away.

"Let's go." Jase rushed back for them and the backpacks.

Mochi took her hand and held on tight. She made a low, soothing sound. "We'll be okay." And she moved forward, not letting on that her knees were shaking.

Sure, she knew that she'd always been surrounded by violence in the camp. But this was the first time she saw any of it up close and personal. She'd do well to remember that Jase wasn't just a good ol' boy from Texas. He was very much one of Pedro's men. She held her gun tight as she moved forward in the cover of the darkness.

She couldn't see the breach until they were just a few feet away. Someone had carefully snipped the aluminum wire. She had a pretty good idea who that had been.

"Where are we going?" she whispered, wondering if she was jumping from the pot into the fire.

"North. Time to see about a new job."

North worked for her. The research station was that way.

Jase helped Mochi through the hole first, then held the wire back with his bare hands to help her pass through.

. She angled her body. The contortionist act would have been much easier if she didn't have a beach ball attached to her midriff, but she made it through. She was going to be as tough as she needed to be. She was going to survive this.

Then she was outside the compound for the first time in months. She glanced behind her, her muscles tight with tension. But she didn't see anyone back there. Nobody seemed to realize what they'd just done.

She was free.

She straightened her spine and drew a deep breath, looked up to the sky. No man was ever going to control her again. Her fingers tightened on the gun as she looked at Jase's back. He'd already turned his attention to the forest and was moving rapidly forward into deeper cover.

Mochi turned back to her with a look of concern, as though to make sure she was all right.

She flashed him a smile. "We'll be okay." And the boy nodded, as they both hustled forward.

She watched where she stepped, wary of snakes and spiders. She might not spot them in the dark. Some of the plants, too, were poisonous, but she didn't know all of them, only a couple. She hoped Jase did, and wouldn't lead them into something that could kill them.

Okay, so he'd broken her out. But she was pretty sure he wasn't helping her out of the goodness of his heart. Chances were, he'd gotten cold feet and just wanted to avoid the battle, deciding to sit it out in the jungle than pledge allegiance to the winner. He was probably only bringing her with him for entertainment, since she'd done her best to pretend the last time they'd met that she wouldn't mind entertaining him.

"Where are Cristobal's men?" she asked, wary of running into them.

"Still some distance away, I'd guess."

"The explosion?"

"I needed a distraction."

"Where are we going?"

"Away from the fighting."

"More specifically?"

"Plenty of logging down river where a man can find a job. Other kinds of work, too." He didn't mention what she would be doing. Did he plan on making her his camp woman?

Mochi looked back again to check on her. Again, she did her best to reassure him with a smile. She wasn't sure why the boy was with them. Maybe Jase hoped the kid would help them navigate the jungle. She hoped the same. Her chances of reaching safety would triple if she could get Mochi to help her.

Truthfully, as long as she had Mochi, she didn't really need Jase, who was at least as big a threat as help, if not bigger.

The boy held a branch aside so it wouldn't hit her belly.

"*Gracias,* Mochi."

She padded deeper into the forest behind them, and after the first couple of yards the undergrowth thinned enough so she could see better in what little moonlight filtered in through the canopy. She weighed the gun in her hand and lifted it, pointed the barrel at Jase's back as he moved carefully ahead in the semidarkness. She hesitated for a long moment, then adjusted her aim at his right shoulder. Newfound resolution or not, she didn't think she could kill a man in cold blood.

Not unless it became absolutely necessary.

Which wasn't the case right now. He'd gotten her away from camp; now she just needed to get away from him. She didn't have to kill him for that. She hoped.

She moved up closer behind Mochi, who walked between her and Jase. The kid barely reached her nonexistent waist. She couldn't possibly hit him as long as she aimed well over his head.

Deep breath. Her finger hesitated on the trigger. Not because of that kiss they'd shared, she told herself. But if she shot Jase now, the sound of gunfire might draw some of Don Pedro's men to them.

She'd have plenty of opportunity to shoot the guy later. First, she might as well let him lead them a safe distance from the camp. But then she was taking control.

She drew a long breath and lowered the weapon.

"I was about to recommend that," Jase said without turning around, his tone mild. "That old thing has about the same chance of hitting me as blowing up in your hands."

Chapter Five

Jase scanned the forest in front of them. Not that he could see worth a damn. Couldn't hear too much, either; the usual jungle noises drowned out pretty much everything. Moisture dripped from leaves, a startled bird cried here and there. The bugs just plain never shut up. As far as they were concerned, the jungle was theirs.

He also paid attention to what was going on behind him. Melanie had backed down with the whole gun thing. Good. He wasn't sure exactly how he would have tackled a pregnant woman.

He'd been pretty sure she wouldn't shoot him. He was a fair judge of character. But even if she did pull the trigger, chances were she would have missed in the dark. In any case, his most important organs were protected by the back wall of the backpack that he'd lined with Kevlar before he'd headed off to find Don Pedro almost a year ago.

That she'd considered taking a shot gave him hope. It meant she had enough courage and grit, which boded well for her chances of making it to the research station.

Jase picked up the pace, calling over his shoulder, "Let me know when you need a break."

"How long, do you think, before they realize that we're gone?"

"They'll figure out in about ten minutes that the enemy isn't here yet and the explosion had nothing to do with Cristobal. Then they'll search the camp for an explanation. They'll be slowed by the darkness. A couple of hours might pass before they find Jorge's body and the hole in the fence. Then they'll have to figure out who is missing. I think they'll wait until morning to track us, but by then the enemy will be here, so they'll have bigger problems."

"We shouldn't stop anyway, for a while. Just in case," she said. "I'd rather be a safe distance from camp."

"Nothing's safe about cutting through the jungle at night." The trek was downright suicidal, in fact, yet still better than remaining at camp and awaiting battle.

He almost missed the faint animal trail in the dark. He slowed and looked again, then pulled his trusty, worn compass from his pocket and flicked on his flashlight. They'd exited the camp on the west side, but he turned north now, following the trail that seemed to lead that way.

Cristobal and his men would come from the east. Better avoid that bunch, if possible.

They plodded forward in silence for a while, his flashlight illuminating a narrow path in front of them. They were far enough from camp now that the light should be safe. It did draw a host of insects, however, that seemed to be eating them alive. Still, a little blood loss was nothing compared to stepping on a pit viper.

He glanced back after a while. "You two okay?"

"Fine." A light scarf protected Melanie's face and neck. She swatted at the bugs.

The insects didn't seem to bother the boy. He was used to running through the jungle in nothing but a loincloth. He had more covering now than he'd ever seen in his life. He proudly wore the linen shirt and shorts Consuela had made him, going to great pains to keep them clean. Not an easy task in the jungle.

The dog bite on his arm would have to be checked in the morning, when there was more light, Jake thought. He kept the pace manageable, holding back for the sake of the other two. On his own he could have made the trek to the research station in a day. But as things stood…Mochi was used to the jungle terrain, but his legs were too short to walk too fast. And Melanie would need regular periods of rest.

With the rough terrain they would be lucky to cover ten miles a day, which meant three days there. He'd drop them off, then come back to camp. The fight could very well still be going. The compound had been strategically built; the Don's men could easily dig themselves in and hold off a larger force for a good long time. Jase could pretend that he'd been captured by the enemy at the beginning and had just broken free, returning to rejoin the melee. He'd deny having seen Mochi and Melanie or that he had anything to do with their disappearance.

Or, if the fight was over and Cristobal had won, Jase could slink into camp and ask the new boss to take him in, swear allegiance to the new guy. Then he could continue with his intelligence gathering. However it played out, he planned on finishing his mission and accomplishing what he'd come here to do.

He pushed forward as briskly as he could safely do

so, and the bugs dropped back after a while. Thank God for small mercies.

He looked back periodically as he walked to make sure nobody fell behind. He needn't have worried. Both Melanie and Mochi kept up. They knew what was at stake.

He kept listening for noises indicating they were being followed. But neither his senses nor his instincts signaled danger, so after a while he relaxed. Then tensed again when he considered that as little ground as they'd covered so far, it might already be too much for Melanie.

"How far along are you?" He found the question uncomfortable, but asked it anyway.

"Eight months."

He winced. She didn't look that far along. But what did he know about pregnant women, anyway? Absolutely nothing. And he would have been damned happy to keep things that way.

Okay. All right. Not a problem. Three days, four at the most, and he would deliver her to the research station where she could be flown out in the next chopper that brought supplies. She would be fine. He'd leave Mochi there, too, and would come back for the kid later, after the battle was over and his position at camp was secure once again. Then he'd find the boy a suitable village.

He ordered the first rest stop after forty minutes or so, way too early.

"I can go longer," she insisted, but she had both hands at her lower back, supporting the extra weight she carried.

"How about I take that gun?" he offered, his motives not entirely altruistic.

She hesitated a lot longer than he would have liked, but did hand the weapon over in the end, probably aware that he could have taken it away from her if he wanted to, anyway.

"Even seasoned soldiers sit out the dark." He put away the old pistol and pulled their canteens from his backpack, then handed them out. "Drink."

They wouldn't eat at this stop. That could wait until morning.

He checked their three days' worth of food, enough to last them to their destination, to make sure no bugs had gotten into it. He planned on scavenging on his way back, to cut down on the weight he had to carry.

When he checked everything to his satisfaction and found no problems, he picked up his own canteen and panned his flashlight around as he drank, scanning the immediate area. Glowing eyes reflected back the light here and there.

Melanie pulled closer to him on the log they all shared, and he caught a whiff of her shampoo, something citrusy. "What are those?"

"Mostly monkeys. You can tell a jaguar apart by the shape of his cat eyes."

"But big cats are fewer and fewer in the world's jungles, right?"

"Sure." No need to share the story of him coming face-to-face with a tiger in the jungles of Sumatra on a night very much like this. He'd been saving a journalist the guerillas had taken hostage. No connection to his mission at the time whatsoever. Took a bullet in the leg for her, too. They still kept in touch. Audrey and her family—husband and kids—sent him a Christmas card every year.

The need to protect the weak, to stand up for women and kids, ran deep in his Texas blood. He couldn't help it.

"How far have we come?" Melanie asked.

Not nearly far enough. "Don't worry about it. We'll cover more ground once the sun comes up."

"Do you think Mochi can handle the walk? How did his arm get hurt?" She was looking at the bandage that was partially concealed by the boy's shirt, as if she'd just noticed it. The way Jase had set the flashlight down partially illuminated the boy.

"A dog bit him." Better not elaborate on that story either. She had way too much stress to deal with already, not a good thing for a woman in her condition. "He walked everywhere his whole life so far. They have no cars or even bicycles in the jungle villages. I promise you, he can take whatever you can take." Probably more, actually, under the circumstances.

She kept her gaze on the boy, who was playing with the puppy.

Jase kept his gaze on her. That she worried more about Mochi than herself said something about her.

He stopped that train of thought right there. Helping her was one thing; starting to like her was a complication he didn't need.

He put away his water and stood to gather some firewood. Of course, with the high humidity and on-and-off rain, everything dripped with moisture.

He shaved some deadwood with his knife and used the dry core to help him light a couple of thin branches.

That provided enough heat to set a larger chunk of wood on fire. "This should help with the wild animals."

She looked around at the dark forest as she wrapped her arms around her torso. "About those jaguars…"

"They could be around." No sense in giving her false security. Better if they were all prepared for everything. "But not common. It all depends on whether or not we'll be crossing one's territory."

They fell silent for a while. Mochi shared his drink with the puppy, pulled the dog on his lap, then pulled his legs up and wrapped his arms around his knees, lay his head down and fell asleep. The crackling of the fire and the night sounds of the jungle filled the air.

A howler monkey cried out in the distance.

Maybe it had met up with a snake. Jase kept his eyes on their surroundings to make sure they avoided that fate.

The puppy wiggled away from Mochi. The boy snatched it back.

Nobody was going to get any sleep that way. Jase took off his belt and cut off a narrow strip of leather, bored a hole with his pocket knife and made a makeshift dog collar. Then he hunted for a slim but strong green vine that would be flexible enough to make a good leash. He tied the dog to a sapling when he was done.

"So what's the story with the puppy?" Melanie asked, watching him.

"Damn nuisance." He had no idea why he'd agreed to take the dog along. Temporary insanity.

He was in the middle of a crucial op. And he had managed to collect a jungle kid, a pregnant woman and a three-legged puppy.

She smiled at him for the first time since he'd busted into her room.

He refused to let that smile affect him on any level. He looked away.

"Have you been working for Pedro long?"

"Almost a year."

She'd been at the camp for only a few months. He'd heard about the woman up at the hacienda, but had never seen her before he'd caught her crying on the balcony. He'd spent most of his time in the jungle running errands with one group or another. Since he'd been on probation, working to gain the Don's trust, he hadn't been allowed up at the house before that. And even if he had been, from what she'd said, the Don liked to keep her under lock and key.

"What did you do before coming here?" she asked next.

"This and that. I even piloted a riverboat on the Amazon once." He couldn't help a grin. Those were good memories—an undercover op that had lasted six months and made a considerable dent in the drug trade.

"And you…" she hesitated, her smile fading "…like this work?"

He extended his hands toward the fire. "It's pretty much the only thing I'm good at."

Something flashed across her gaze. He couldn't tell by the low light of the flames whether it was regret or disappointment. For a second he wished he could tell her the truth about himself. *Too risky.* She'd be out of his hair in a few days, anyway. They'd likely never see each other again. What she thought of his moral turpitude didn't matter.

He was pretty sure he could hand her off without having to break his cover. That was the plan, anyway.

He would trek right by the research station, announcing to her that they had to go around it carefully. Then let her slip away from him and take Mochi with her, as she would no doubt try the first chance she got. She would escape to safety, and he could turn around and go back to camp to finish his work.

Minutes ticked on. Their clothes were slowly drying, the night a little more comfortable as they warmed up.

He gave the boy another ten minutes to sleep, then touched the kid's shoulder to wake him. He was prepared to carry Mochi if he had to. But the boy's eyes snapped open and he immediately went for the dog. Then he began marching down the trail, carrying the puppy in his arms, despite the leash. He knew the forest well enough to know that snakes were a danger to a little puppy who would just love to stray off the trail if given too much slack.

"Let me know if you see or hear anything out there," he told the boy in Spanish.

Mochi gave a smile. He seemed to be doing well. And he trusted Jase.

Melanie didn't trust him, though. Jase noticed that she kept a close, wary eye on him.

They kept going on the narrow trail and were soon soaked to the skin again, even though it wasn't raining. They brushed up against wet leaves constantly, and moisture dripped from above, too. Along with all kinds of bugs. He had his jungle hat, Melanie had her scarf. Mochi's head was shaved, so whatever fell on it slid right off. He didn't seem to be bothered by the bugs anyway. He was a pretty easygoing, happy little kid.

He'd seen the boy sad from time to time in the past day or so, probably thinking about his family, but his spirits were up for the most part. Mochi had accepted the loss and lived very much in the present, probably used to staggering losses, living as he did in a very dangerous corner of the jungle.

Life expectancy couldn't be more than thirty, maybe forty years among the natives. The boy had already learned that special attitude of the tribes to take the bad with the good and live every moment as if it was a gift.

Back in the U.S., harried business executives paid thousands of dollars for special retreats to teach them the same thing, Jase thought with some irony.

He kept track of the time, and in another half hour stopped for another break. Again, Mochi was quickly asleep. Jase made another fire, although he wouldn't have bothered if he'd traveled by himself.

Melanie kept watching him. Probably trying to figure out why he'd broken her out of camp. If he wasn't careful, she might figure out that he wasn't who he said he was.

"I expect to be paid for this," he told her.

She glanced at his backpack where he'd stashed her pistol. "Pedro doesn't let me keep money."

He wondered if she'd offer kisses again, and prayed he had the strength to turn them down if she did. Bad enough he'd let that happen once.

But she didn't try anything like that. She didn't say a word, just looked uncomfortable and worried.

"You're an American. There's always a reward." He shrugged, playing the mercenary.

"There is!" She grabbed on to that immediately, obviously lying through her teeth. She didn't have much of a poker face. "My father will be very grateful."

There was a good chance she didn't even have a father. But he gave her points for quick thinking. If he truly *was* a mercenary, that was exactly what he would have wanted to hear. "Well." He gave a swarthy smile. "We have a plan then."

She seemed relieved and even dozed off after another couple of minutes. The fire cast shadows on her face. She was beautiful in any light. He caught himself and looked away.

He picked up a small branch and whittled it down to a peg to keep himself busy, cut another strip of leather off his belt and played with that a little, trying to think how he could best fit the two together.

He let the woman and the boy rest for half an hour, then woke them gently. Mochi came instantly awake. She needed more coaxing, but got there eventually. She moved without protest, rubbing her belly.

"We'll walk a little farther, then make camp for the night. We should be far enough by then to be safe." They needed rest so they could cover a decent distance once the sun came up.

"How are you doing with the bug bites?" He'd noticed her scratching earlier.

"My hands are the worst."

She had softer skin than he did. He thought for a second, kicked aside the decaying leaf mold under his feet until he got to dirt, then he bent and scooped up some muddy soil. "Give me your hands."

She did.

And he rubbed mud all over them. "This should help a little."

Rubbing her slim fingers sent unexpected awareness through him. Man, he'd been alone too long when just holding a woman's hand turned him on. *Pitiful.*

He let her go and busied himself ruffling the puppy so she wouldn't guess how touching her had affected him.

"Thank you," she said, her voice a little thicker than usual.

"Just don't forget to wash it off before you eat." He gave the dog one last pat then picked up their bags and strode forward on the trail.

Three days.

It'd probably be best if he didn't touch her again.

A SHRILL BIRD call woke Melanie toward dawn. The fire burned low in the middle of their small campsite. It had been enough to keep predators away overnight. And the smoke did cut down on the number of insects, although not nearly enough. She was more than grateful for the mosquito netting over her sleeping bag. Thank God, Jase had thought of everything when he'd packed his bag.

She rubbed the sleep from her eyes and watched as he slipped from his sleeping bag and stirred the fire. He stood tall, his body well-built, his senses already alert as he observed their surroundings. He had a straight nose and a square, masculine jaw, but her attention only skimmed those, settling on his lips. And for a moment, she could feel his mouth against hers all over again.

Ridiculous that she couldn't forget that brief moment. Troubling that tingles pinged through her body just from the memory.

He stirred the embers to get enough heat to boil water

for coffee, but he didn't add more wood. They would be leaving shortly.

He looked her way once he set the tin cup on the fire, his gunmetal-gray gaze catching hers. "I'm going to refill our canteens. I heard a creek not far off the trail when we stopped last night. I'm checking it out. Stay here."

She couldn't believe her luck. "Okay."

She waited until he disappeared in the bushes, then left her sleeping bag and began gathering up things that she would need for her journey. She took Jase's backpack, since it was bigger than hers, and left some of the food on a stone by the fire, hoping the ants wouldn't find it before he did. She owed him some consideration. He *had* helped her. So far.

Some of the tension in her back eased. Leaving him without having to shoot him was so much nicer and easier. She'd been worried about that, if she could pull the trigger, if she could somehow steal her pistol back in the first place. She'd worried about what Mochi would think of her, seeing her shoot the man the boy clearly admired. Jase simply walking off and leaving them alone lifted a tremendous weight off her shoulders.

She tried to free her sleeping bag from the tree, but couldn't cope with the complicated knots Jase had tied, so as much as she hated to, she had to leave that behind. She did pack the mosquito netting. She also found the pistol and kept it handy in case he came back too soon. She prayed that he wouldn't.

Would the old weapon really blow up in her hands if she fired it? Could be he'd just been trying to discourage her. A working gun would have made her feel safer as she walked through the jungle. Jase had taken his gun with him, but she wouldn't have known what to do with that anyway. His sinister black weapon looked twice as complicated as the old-fashioned pistol she had. She did take the machete, though, which she would definitely need.

The lack of safe-filter canteens worried her the most. Jase had taken those. Mochi and she would need water. But it did rain regularly, and she reasoned that rainwater straight from the sky would have to be safe to drink. There couldn't be any parasites in that. Hopefully she could gather some of that from the larger leaves.

She strapped the bag onto her back. "Let's go, Mochi."

The boy looked at her wide-eyed, then looked in the direction where Jase had disappeared.

"We have to go now." She walked over to him and picked up the puppy in an ungainly sweep. The furry little thing settled right against her, practically sitting on her shelf of a belly. "Come on. It's going to be better this way. Trust me."

Mochi dragged his feet, but then followed at last, not wanting to be separated from the puppy.

She followed the same trail they'd been using until now, grateful when another one crossed it. This gave her a fifty percent chance that Jase might take the wrong path when he followed them. She looked up at the sun. One of the trails headed straight north, the other northwest.

Did he know about the research station to the north? If he did, would he think that she did, too, and she would head straight that way? She took the northwest branch to be on the safe side, deciding to cut over later. She should be able to figure this out.

"We'll be fine," she told Mochi, walking carefully.

She'd spent enough time at camp so that the jungle noises no longer scared her. Plus, she gained courage from the machete she was holding. Still, when a loud crack and thud sounded in the distance, she nearly jumped out of her skin, even if she had heard the sound before and knew it to be harmless.

"A tree falling," she explained to Mochi, who didn't seem the least concerned.

He pointed to the nearest tree then reenacted the falling part with a grin. Okay. They were definitely on the same page. Of course, he would know the forest better than she did. She had a genuine native guide with her.

The constant humidity of the jungle eroded wood fairly quickly. One of Pedro's top men had been killed by a falling tree in the jungle shortly after she'd gotten here. The others had brought in the body and she'd seen it from the balcony, not something she would forget anytime soon. So in addition to watching where she stepped, she also paid attention to the trees.

"Ay!" Mochi grabbed her from behind suddenly.

The puppy yelped in her arms.

Right. She needed to pay attention to the bushes, too. She'd nearly walked into a bright red snake. Judging by the way Mochi gave wide berth to the thing, it had to be fairly deadly.

She shuddered as she moved on. "*Gracias,* Mochi."

The boy stood taller and said something back in his own language. From the tone of his voice and his body language, she guessed he was promising to take good care of her.

"We'll take good care of each other," she told him,

and moved forward, trying to keep an eye on absolutely everything.

She did really well for the first twenty minutes. Then they came to an area where vegetation was thicker. Time for the machete. She handed the puppy to Mochi. Leading it on the leash would have slowed them down too much, as it would want to stop and investigate absolutely every ant and leaf. Plus there was no telling what might dart out from the undergrowth to snatch it.

She was a little more frazzled around the edges, more jittery, without Jase.

She needed both hands to work the machete. She went at it like she meant it. Wow. Clearing a path looked a lot easier when Jase had done it. Her arms were ready to fall off in about five minutes.

A little more and she would stop to drink. She monitored her level of exhaustion, watched for any unusual pain, but her body didn't seem to mind the exercise. She'd been cooped up too long at the hacienda.

"I can do this," she reassured Mochi, then raised the machete above her head, brought it down, then did it over and over again. Until she suddenly couldn't.

The blade got stuck in something above her head.

She looked up, sweaty and annoyed. Her heart about stopped at the sight that greeted her.

She'd managed to hit a hornets' nest that hung low on a branch above the trail, hidden among the leaves.

All was quiet for a second. She didn't move. She didn't dare breathe. Then the nest began to vibrate.

"Run!" she yelled, but Mochi was already tearing into the woods, off the trail.

She dropped the backpack and followed him with an uneven gait, holding on to her belly.

The hornets followed her, a whole cloud of the furious colony. They were catching up quickly. No surprise there. A kitchen chair could have outrun her these days.

The first few stings came right through her clothing. She zigzagged with an alacrity she wouldn't have thought she still possessed, dashed through bushes just to brush the damned things off. Ran to the left, then ran to the right, having no idea how to escape, running blindly and quickly losing sight of Mochi, who blended into the undergrowth too well.

She needed to catch her breath. Her lungs burned from the short burst of effort. Her skin burned from the stings. It didn't seem possible that things could go this bad this quickly.

And then everything got a lot worse. A hornet stung her right on her eyelid, making her yelp with pain. Her eye swelled shut in less than thirty seconds.

She kept her other hand up by the other eye, swatting whatever came that way. If anything happened to that eye, she would be completely blind. And then she would probably be dead very shortly after. Either the hornets would get her, or the snakes, or she'd fall over something and break her neck.

"Whatever you concentrate on is what's going to happen," Julio used to tell her. "So concentrate on good things."

So she tried to think of making it out of here and being back in her apartment in Rio. But she got stung on the other eyelid anyway. She cried out, heading into the thickest bush to hide from the hornets, peering through a narrowing gap until finally she couldn't see anything.

Oh, dear Lord, help me!

She hurt all over, unable to tell if she was being stung

over and over or if the pain came from her old stings. She could definitely hear the hornets buzzing. She felt tears run down her face.

Every time she moved and a leaf brushed against her, she thought it was a snake. She wanted to scream for help, but Jase was far away, and she didn't want to draw Mochi to herself and have the hornets attack him.

She curled into a ball, as much as she was able to, her head down and her arms wrapped around it to protect her face. She needed a plan, but she couldn't think.

She tried to keep calm. Stress would be bad for her baby. Stress could even induce labor.

Oh, God, don't think of that.

Think of a solution.

But the only image she could call up was Jase's face, and the ease with which he handled even the most difficult things.

Black-hearted mercenary or not, she wished she hadn't run away from him.

Chapter Six

Minutes passed. If she were allergic, she would be dead by now. But she wasn't, and she gave thanks for that mercy.

Melanie stiffened as she heard a slight noise, maybe a small animal, somewhere close by. Then the sound of dribbling water. The smell of ammonia hit her nose.

"Señora?" Mochi's small hand settled on her shoulder a few seconds later, followed by Chico's barking at her feet.

"Run, Mochi!"

Then something cool touched her skin, moist and sticky. He was packing something on her, mud, from the feel of it. She could have cried in relief.

"Melanie!" Jase's voice called from the distance.

Mochi responded first. *"Aquí, señor. Aquí!"*

"There are hornets. Don't come any closer!" Melanie shouted.

But he was there anyway, a second or two later, his voice clipped with anger as he said, *"Gracias,* Mochi."

In another second she smelled smoke. Right next to her, filling her nose. She coughed, covered her nose and mouth. Soon the buzzing lessened, then died away.

"I struck their nest." She felt incredibly stupid. Now

she was really at his mercy, and he was probably mad at her for taking off. Way to make a bad situation worse.

"Move carefully to the left," he told her. "You're next to an anthill."

She swallowed hard.

"Looks like Mochi laid down a line of urine to keep them at bay."

She expected him to yell at her. Julio would have done that. He'd been a sweet guy 90 percent of the time, but he'd had that hot South American temper. And from time to time he'd lost it. She pulled her neck in, ready for Jase to let his own temper loose on her.

"I saw the machete," he said evenly. "You hit one pretty big nest. Are you okay?" He took her hand, his fingers gentle on her skin.

His touch reached something deep inside her. "I can't see."

"Other than your eyes, where are you stung?"

He probably couldn't see the stings because of the mud. She pointed at a dozen different places. "Why does it hurt so much?" She moaned the words, she couldn't help it.

"Hornet venom has about five percent of acetylcholine. It's not like a garden-variety bee sting." He let her hand go, and she wished he hadn't. "I'm going to scrape out their stingers with the back of my knife. Hang in there for a minute."

He took her face between his palms. "Actually, let me start with those eyelids."

He used his fingernail, from the feel of it.

When he was done he moved on to the rest of her body, including her scalp. Every single bite pulsed with burning pain. After he finished he packed more wet mud on her skin.

She tried to picture him fussing over her bites. Tried to picture herself. With her belly, she had to look like a hippo on her way home from mud bathing.

"Here, drink."

Something cold touched her lips. Probably the canteen.

She drank her fill while he tied a cool, wet cloth around her eyes. "That should bring down the swelling."

"Thank you."

He didn't respond, and she had no idea what he was doing once he let her go. "We'll rest here awhile," he said after a minute.

She thought about that. She'd had a chance to catch her breath while he'd been treating her. The sooner they got going, the sooner they'd reach the research station.

"We should go." None of her stings would hurt any less sitting than walking. "If you're willing to lead me."

He helped her up, his strong hands taking hers, pulling her up easily. "The second you need to rest, you tell me," he declared, firmly back in command.

She was dismayed to find that she was actually relieved. Then she decided to cut herself a little slack. She'd get right back on her quest for independence as soon as she could see again.

"Did the hornets sting Mochi?"

"He looks fine. Chico is good, too."

She moved forward, aware of her complete dependence on him. She had to trust him to help her, when she'd just sworn not long ago that she would never trust another man again, especially not someone like Jase.

Blind trust. She finally knew the full meaning of

the words, not that she wanted to. The concept scared her. She had a tendency to trust the wrong kind of man. That was how she'd ended up in this godforsaken jungle in the first place.

And Jase was definitely the wrong kind of man, just like Pedro, her brother-in-law, even if on a smaller scale.

All the little niceties he'd done for her flashed into her mind. She pushed the images away.

He had to be the same as the others at camp to work for someone like Pedro. She couldn't start wishing for some fairy tale, then start believing it. She'd done that with Julio and that had ended pretty badly.

She wasn't going to fall for Jase's temporary kindness. She would follow him until she recovered her vision, then she would get away from him again as soon as they neared the research station. This time, more carefully. In the meanwhile, she could work on making him forget her first attempt, make him trust her once again.

"I'm sorry I left." The pure truth, no lying there.

A moment of silence passed, his grip on her hand tightening slightly. "This can't happen again. You could have killed yourself. You put each of us at risk."

"I was scared. I don't know where you're going. What if someone there will take me straight back to Pedro in hopes of a reward?" She swallowed. All he'd told her was that he was off seeking other employment somewhere up north.

Silence stretched between them.

"You can trust me," he said at last.

She couldn't trust him, obviously, but she didn't want to insult him. He'd just saved her life. "My father will be very grateful to you. He's well off, financially."

Her father had been dead for years and had always

been an underpaid educator. But she had to give Jase some incentive. "As soon as you take me to civilization, I'll contact him."

Another stretch of silence followed.

"You don't have to run away from me," he said at last. "I'm not who you think I am."

Even the worst criminals often had delusions like that, she reflected. Pedro fancied himself as some godfather-like figure who gave work to hundreds. He thought himself strict but benevolent. He was a folk hero in his own mind, helping the poor and evading the government.

"You do what you have to. You don't really have another choice." She made sure to sound accepting and understanding.

He muttered something she couldn't make out. Sounded like he was swearing under his breath. Okay, here it came. The yelling. She'd tried to do the opposite, but somehow she'd managed to make him angry at her anyway. She couldn't afford that at this stage.

She wrapped her free arm around her belly. "Please don't be mad at me." She needed his help to survive.

"I'm not mad." He stopped walking. Fell silent for a minute before he spoke again, his voice grave. "I work for the U.S. government. So please, don't run away again. I'm your best bet here."

Sure he was.

He must have read the skepticism on her mud-covered face, because he continued, "I've been doing undercover work at the Don's compound."

It surprised her how much she wanted that to be true. She wanted him to be different from the rest. She wanted to believe that she was safe with him. She could talk herself into believing him so, so easily. Which was why she had to make sure she didn't do that. She had to use common sense.

"You don't believe me." Frustration rang through his voice.

"I do," she lied. She was blind and completely dependent on staying in his good graces.

"Okay. Doesn't matter. The important thing is that I'm going to take care of you. All right? Whether you believe it or not. All you have to do is hang on to my hand and follow me." He started walking again.

She did what he told her, her mind buzzing. Okay, he *was* somehow different from the rest of the men at camp, and he *had* busted her out. She supposed she could give him the benefit of the doubt.

"So you came to the camp because of the drugs?" She might not have been allowed in the packaging building, but she wasn't stupid.

"That, and because Don Pedro is now supplying weapons to terrorists. We also think his human smuggling ring is planning to smuggle terrorists into the U.S. There've been movements of some suspicious payments into his Swiss accounts. I don't suppose you know anything about that."

The words hit her square in the chest. Everything inside her railed to deny what she was hearing. She didn't want to believe that someone she was related to—even if only by marriage—would do something like this.

But why would Jase make it up? What would he have to gain?

Try as she might, she couldn't come up with a satisfying answer to those questions. And when she considered all she'd seen from Pedro and all she'd seen from

Jase, she was tempted to believe Jase over her brother-in-law any day of the week.

Pedro was capable of involving himself in absolutely anything that promised to make him money. He considered himself above the law. He thought he was invincible.

But making a deal with terrorists…

Oh, God.

She just found a whole bunch of new incentives to make sure that she got herself and her baby as far as possible from her brother-in-law, to do whatever she could to make sure he would never find them again.

Of course, first she had to survive the next couple of days.

"Who do you work for?" she asked. "Are you some kind of special forces?" She didn't have a lot of trouble picturing that, actually.

Bringing the kid and the puppy along made more sense in that light. Any mercenary might think that they'd get a reward for an American like her. But a mercenary wouldn't save Mochi from camp, and certainly not a three-legged puppy.

He moved slowly as he led her, making sure she could keep up. "I can't really talk about this. I only said what I said to make sure you won't run away again."

She made no promises. She wanted to believe him, and she did to a point, but fully trusting anyone didn't come easily just now. "Is Jase your real name?"

"Yes."

Okay. That was something. "Are you really from Texas?"

"Wouldn't lie about that, no, ma'am. Who'd want to be from anyplace else, anyway?"

That sounded about right, spoken like a true Texan. She felt better hearing the grin in his voice. "Where are you really taking me?"

"To a research station not far away. Apparently, a chopper comes monthly with supplies and fresh staff. They can take you out of here."

Dear God, let that be true. "And you?"

"I go back to doing what I've been doing."

Her mind buzzed with questions more specific to his mission, but she was pretty sure he wouldn't answer any of those, so she followed him silently, trying to ignore the pain and the stink of the mud that covered her face.

He held her hand firmly and made sure she didn't fall every time she stumbled. "I'm going to make sure you get out of here all right."

She wanted to believe him.

Her bunched-up muscles were starting to ache. She needed to relax. She couldn't. She found walking through the jungle nerve-wracking on her best day. Walking through the jungle blind was downright terrifying.

But the touch of Jase's hand, his long fingers folded around hers, anchored her, kept her from panicking. If he really was who he claimed…

She thought of the clumsy way she'd tried to seduce him back at the hacienda and embarrassment washed over her.

"I'm so sorry for kissing you." She blurted the words without thinking, embarrassing herself all over again.

A long moment of silence passed, during which she wanted to sink into the earth. She hated that she couldn't see his face.

"Don't ever apologize for a kiss like that." His voice held amusement.

"I thought—"

"I know what you thought. We're okay on that. Believe me. No man on earth would complain about that kiss."

She drew a quick breath, flustered. "Probably no need to talk about it at all, then." *Please, God.*

"Can I at least think about it?" His voice held a grin again.

She was sure her cheeks were fire-engine red. Her only hope was that he couldn't tell with all her stings and all the mud.

"If I don't overdo it?" He pushed. "Maybe just once or twice an hour?"

And then, against all odds, she found herself smiling, some of her pent-up tension disappearing. "You can think of whatever you want if you guarantee that we won't run into any more hornets."

He was silent for a few seconds. "The thing to do in a bee or hornet attack is to get in water, if there's any nearby. Submerge yourself completely for as long as you can. They do give up after a while." He kept talking, as if he knew that hearing his voice soothed her, somehow made up for her lost sense of sight. "Or go into a very dark place. Like the back of a cave. Bees can't see in the dark."

He must have learned that in some jungle-survival training class, she decided, glad that he was prepared for all the hazards that faced them.

"Is this side trip going to mess up your mission?" she asked, as the thought occurred to her. And realized that she believed him more with every passing minute.

"How are you going to explain taking me and Mochi out of camp when you go back to Pedro?"

"I'll find a way to make it work."

But she wondered if he only said that so she wouldn't feel bad about derailing his undercover operation. "Are there others like you at camp?"

He stayed silent.

Of course, he probably couldn't tell her anything about that.

"Sorry. I shouldn't have asked."

"I'm the only one," he said at last.

He would say that either way, she figured. Bad enough that his cover was blown, he wouldn't betray a teammate. Although, she was tempted to think that he was telling the truth. She'd seen most of the men who worked for Don Pedro, and she hadn't seen anyone remotely like Jase.

Putting one foot in front of the other blindly was as scary as anything she'd ever done, but she trusted him more with every passing second, and was soon walking forward without thinking too much about it. She had the overwhelming feeling that he *would* keep her safe.

And she was pitifully grateful for that, if not a little disappointed that she'd gotten herself into this situation in the first place.

"I was going to take care of myself," she voiced her thoughts out loud. "I shouldn't have to rely on you for everything. This was supposed to be my big break for independence," she added, unable to help the irony from her voice. "I was going to grow up before the baby came."

"You're pregnant and blind. In the middle of the jungle. Give yourself a break. And you're plenty grown up already. You survived a bandit camp. Hell, you survived Don Pedro. There are hundreds of rough guys, now dead and buried, who can't make that claim."

"I *am* going to be independent someday. I *can* handle it."

"I have no doubt about that whatsoever. You got away from me, didn't you? Not many people can say that, either, believe me."

His declaration made her feel better.

She hung on to his hand and followed, lifting her feet clear of the ground with each step so she wouldn't trip over anything. Although it felt like an eternity, she was pretty sure half an hour hadn't yet passed when he called for their next break.

"I can walk," she protested immediately. "Walking is the recommended exercise for pregnant women." She scratched her neck, her skin getting itchy now that the sun was higher in the sky and the mud was drying.

"We're close to a creek. We should take advantage of it," he told her.

She couldn't hear water. Wasn't losing one sense supposed to sharpen the others? They walked a little more. Then she did hear a faint trickling at last that grew progressively louder as they got nearer.

He stopped. "Sit here."

She felt her way around, finding what she thought was a large, flat rock. She sat, and he let her hand go. She hadn't been prepared for it. She immediately felt lost.

"I'm going to check the water," he told her, and kept talking. "Nice little creek. Maybe six feet wide. Water is brisk. Wish there were some edible fruits around, but I don't see any."

He spoke to Mochi next, told the kid to look for food.

She focused on his voice and tried not to think of all the possible dangers surrounding her that she couldn't see, like poisonous plants, bugs and snakes.

He came back in two minutes. "I'd like to wash you off."

She would have given anything to feel cold water on her skin. "Okay."

He tugged on her bootlaces. "I'm going to take you in up to your knees. All you have to do is hang on to me."

She was more than ready to wash off the grime and sweat, except— "What about piranhas?" She hesitated.

"Not in a quick little creek like this."

"Parasites?" She didn't worry about only herself, but had to worry about her baby as well. She would put up with any amount of discomfort rather than risk something bad happening to her unborn son.

"Fast-moving water is usually safe. It's the stagnant pools you have to worry about." He worked her boots and socks off, then took her hand again.

She followed him timidly, especially when they reached some smallish rocks, which were wet and slippery.

Then he stopped at last when the water reached just below her knees. "Stand still. I'll take care of everything. Your center of balance is off with that belly. I don't want you to bend down, lose balance and pitch headfirst into the current. Okay?"

When he put it that way, how could she protest? "Did you just call me fat?" she joked to ease her awareness. *The man was about to bathe her!*

"More like curvaceous, in a blessed way."

"Very smooth."

He gave a flat laugh.

She liked the sound of it. His voice lost most of its
South American flavor and sounded a lot more American now, the Texas twang more noticeable. And she
realized that, before, he'd probably talked like the men
in camp just to fit in. But now there was no reason for
pretense.

He removed the cloth from her eyes first. She tried
to open them, but couldn't. Disappointment washed
over her.

"How long am I going to be like this?"

"A couple of hours, at least. Maybe days."

Oh, God. But she appreciated that he gave her the
truth.

He washed her face first, careful with her swollen
eyes, his fingers barely touching her, the cold water
feeling like heaven as it ran down her skin.

Then he washed her hands, her arms, her neck—
probably bringing water in his palms to pour over her.
She couldn't see, only feel. His gentle care felt comforting and intimate at the same time. All sorts of sen-
sations skittered along her skin every time his fingers
brushed against her.

THE MATERIAL OF her light slacks and shirt clung to her
skin, emphasizing her curves. She might as well have
been naked. His body was as hard as it had ever been,
but he ignored that and kept bathing her, knowing the
cold water had to feel good on her burning stings.

Mochi played around in the water a short distance
up the creek, ignoring what must have seemed like a
strange ritual to him. Then he grew bored with that and

ran ashore, searched through the undergrowth with a stick, careful to keep the puppy on a short leash.

A strange little dog, that one. Chico refused to accept his disability and darted around with enviable agility, despite his missing front leg, as in love with Mochi as Mochi was with him.

But the dog and the kid didn't hold Jase's attention for long, not when Melanie stood right in front of him.

He could have kept up playing in the water with her for a good long time. But he wanted her to have plenty of time to sit and rest before they had to get going again. So, after another couple of minutes, he took her hand and led her out of the water, sat her down on the flat stone at the creek's edge, in the sunshine.

He tugged her clothes away from her skin here and there for modesty. She would have done that if she could see. "Let's stay here a little while and give your clothes a chance to dry."

Not that a person could ever completely dry off in the jungle.

Mochi ran over with some kind of a mushroom, smiling wildly. *"Señor?"* He pointed to his own mouth, as if asking permission to eat it.

He'd found it, he could have it. That was only fair. For all Jase knew the mushroom was a local delicacy. He nodded. He didn't worry about the thing being poisonous. Mochi knew the edible plants in the area better than Jase and Melanie put together. They would have to rely on the kid for advice, and not the other way around.

The boy shoved the mushroom into his mouth and chewed it hard, but didn't swallow. He spit the gooey mess into one hand, then stepped up to Melanie and smeared the slop over her eyes before Jase could stop him.

She sniffed the air. "What is it?"

You don't want to know. "Medicine."

"Thank you," she said politely.

Mochi went on to treat the rest of her stings, looking mightily pleased.

MELANIE UNWRAPPED THE cloth from her eyes at the next rest stop. It needed to be wetted again. She tried to open her eyelids, as she'd done every time the cloth came off. And this time she succeeded. They didn't open fully, but they did open a slit. Even that sliver of bright light seemed blinding. She closed her eyes again as relief swept through her.

Then she tried again, more careful this time, holding her hand above her eyes to shade them.

"Hey." Jase smiled at her. She was sitting on a log and he stood just a few feet from her.

That smile was the most wonderful thing she'd ever seen in her life, even if his face was unshaven and his hair a mess, as if he'd been running his fingers through it. None of that detracted from his ruggedly masculine good looks.

He seemed different, and she wasn't sure if she thought so because she was appreciating seeing again, or because now she knew that he wasn't just one of Pedro's thugs, or because she was beginning to like him. They'd been through a thing or two, at this point. Some tenuous links of trust had built between them.

"Can you see me?"

"Yes." She could have jumped up and thrown herself into his arms, she was so happy. But she was well aware what she must have looked like—both body and face swollen out of proportion. So she pulled back instead and closed her eyes to give them a moment of rest from the light.

Then stole a glance again.

This time, her gaze dipped below his face and she registered the rest of his body. He had his shirt off, and soon she could see why. He'd been in the process of pulling a leech off his abdomen. The flat plane of his belly, those ridges of muscle… Hot need punched through her suddenly and caught her off guard, need she hadn't felt since Julio had died.

A completely out-of-place reaction.

How embarrassing.

Dappled sunlight glinted off Jase's tanned skin. A drop of moisture from the branches above landed on his shoulder and ran down, following the contours of his muscles. He looked like a jungle god, while she…

Melanie pushed to her feet and walked away from him before he could notice her ogling him and she embarrassed herself completely.

"I'll make a fire and we'll eat here," he called after her. He had his shirt back on by the time she turned around. Then he repeated his words in Spanish for Mochi's sake, a little louder so as to be heard over Chico, who had started barking at the bushes.

Mochi simply smiled in response, his standard answer to pretty much everything. Not that the boy seemed fond of the camp food that kept coming from Jase's backpack. He preferred fruit he climbed to get himself, and fat white grubs he dug from under the bark of fallen, decomposing trees. He sucked those down as fast as American kids did candy. He didn't seem to understand why Melanie turned down his offer to share each time, but he didn't seem offended. As far as he was concerned, that meant more for him and the puppy.

Jase moved around their small campsite to collect wood. She went to help him, but before she could pick up the first fallen branch, he froze and lifted a hand in warning, his other hand going for his weapon.

Stopping half-bent like that sent a bolt of pain shooting across her lower back. She straightened slowly and stepped back to the edge of the clearing, sank down on a large rock as she listened for any suspicious noise and scanned the forest around them.

Then she did catch some leaves moving in a patch of bushes, in the direction when Jase was staring. She held her breath, not knowing what to expect. The picture of an attacking jaguar flashed in her mind, but when the branches suddenly parted, Alejandro stepped out of his green hiding place.

The man held two guns, one aimed at Jase, the other aimed at her. A terrifying grin spread on his face.

Chapter Seven

"What the hell did you do to her?" Alejandro's eyes narrowed as he gave Melanie a double-take, his face twisting into a grimace.

Not the sort of comment a girl could take as a compliment. She had the sudden urge to cover her face, but the moment didn't allow for vanity. She scanned the ground, her gaze coming to rest on the machete, about equal distance between her and Jase. He only had eyes for Alejandro, the two men squaring off, weapons aimed.

"You yellow-bellied bastard." The man spit on the ground. "You ran from the fight."

"So did you," Jase pointed out with a shrug. "It's between the bosses. I came here to make a decent living without being harassed by the *policía* every day like I was in the city. Why should we have to die just because those two bosses decided to squabble, eh, amigo? We go someplace else," he said, immediately reverting to camp talk. "How about that? You come with us. Plenty of bosses in the jungle. Plenty of work."

"I ain't no traitor." Alejandro spat again. "I'm here to bring Don Pedro's woman back to him." He glanced at her again, but couldn't quite do it without wincing.

How had he caught up to them so fast? Well, okay, she definitely slowed Jase down. Quite a bit. But still. This meant that Pedro must have noticed that she'd gone missing shortly after Jase had broken them out. And Roberto had probably remembered that Jase had been up in her room before. Maybe they'd put two and two together.

The man kicked at Chico—who barked at his feet, having somehow escaped his leash—but missed. Mochi ran over to scoop the dog up and carried it to a safe distance.

"No gringo bastard will outsmart me," Alejandro growled at Jase. Then he gestured with the gun he held on Melanie. "Up. Get over here. You, too," he told the boy.

She stayed where she sat. "I can't. I'm too exhausted. Everything hurts." God's honest truth.

The man scowled at her. "Try harder. I'm here to save you from this *hombre*."

For a second she didn't know what he was talking about, then realized that he thought Jase had kidnapped her. Don Pedro had probably made that claim to save face. He would never admit that she'd run away from him. But if Alejandro took her back, Pedro would punish her in private, about that she had no doubt.

The last thing she wanted was to be saved from Jase, but she kept her mouth shut. Maybe she could use the fact that Alejandro thought she was here under duress to her advantage.

She made a show of pushing herself up. Groaned. She rubbed the side of her belly. "I don't think this is good for the baby." She sank back down. "I can't do it.

Sorry. I need time to rest. He's been pushing me too hard."

Instead of going to Alejandro as ordered, Mochi moved closer to Melanie.

The man's scowl darkened. He hesitated, probably weighing his options. He had to know that if anything happened to the baby while he brought Melanie back to camp, Pedro would blame him.

"We'll wait," he said after a long, tension-filled second.

He stepped closer to Jase, but still held the second gun on her. Either he wasn't 100 percent sure about Pedro's claims of her kidnapping, or he figured that if Jase cared enough about her to kidnap her, he might be kept in check with threats to her life.

The weapon in his right hand was aimed straight between Jase's eyes. "Drop your gun right now."

Jase didn't move.

She hadn't thought he would. He wouldn't allow himself to be disarmed that easily. She reached out and grabbed Mochi's arm, pulled the boy and the puppy closer, ready to roll behind the large rock she was sitting on if bullets started flying.

Alejandro's finger twitched on the trigger.

Jase dropped and rolled in the blink of an eye, ducking behind a tree.

She slid behind the rock at the same time, pulling Mochi and the puppy with her. The baby kicked inside her, protesting the sudden movement. She kept her head down as she patted her belly. *Everything's going to be okay,* she told herself, and tried to keep her breathing steady, tried not to give way to panic.

"You better be ready to die," Alejandro shouted to

Jase from behind a fallen log, the words followed by some choice obscenities. "Don Pedro doesn't forgive. And I don't either. You stole that kid from me."

Jase didn't respond. And as Melanie popped up for a quick peek, she could no longer see him in the spot behind the palm tree.

"Show yourself!" Alejandro screamed, enraged, as if he, too, just noticed that his opponent had gone missing.

He got no response. An eerie silence settled on the jungle around them. The shouting had quieted the animals around. They were smart enough to sense the danger in the air.

Melanie kept hidden. But she could hear as Alejandro began moving, making the bushes rustle. A minute passed before she realized that the man was moving toward her. Still, when his head popped out from behind the leafy branches, she gave a startled cry. Then he lunged forward and landed next to her behind the rock, got down immediately, holding his gun ready.

She crouched low, unsure whether she could get up without help. Jumping up and running away from the man was out of the question. She held Mochi's arm to make sure the boy wouldn't bolt, either. She wouldn't have put it past Alejandro to shoot at the kid.

He called out again without showing himself. Smarter than he looked, obviously. "I got the woman and the kid. How you gonna sell them now?" He jeered. "I got your money."

Mochi burrowed his head against her shoulder, obviously scared of Alejandro as he'd never been of Jase, making her wonder if the man next to them had given the boy reason to fear him. She folded her arms around the little boy who'd stolen his way into her heart with his cheerful smiles and resilience. Nobody would hurt Mochi, not if she had anything to do with it.

Then something moved in the bushes to their right.

Alejandro aimed his gun that way. She held Mochi closer, her heart lurching into a mad rhythm.

Oh, God, don't let Jase get hurt.

Endless minutes ticked by. No other movement or sound came from that direction. It might have been just a snake or some other small animal.

Maybe Jase had taken off. The dark thought hit her out of nowhere. Mochi and she had nothing to do with his mission. Saving them was nothing but an inconvenient detour for him. He didn't have to risk his life for two strangers.

One of whom had been less than grateful, admittedly. She'd stolen his supplies and left him in the jungle just this morning. She'd been nothing but trouble, slowing him down, mistrusting him.

Yet, something deep inside her told her that he wouldn't abandon them. Ridiculous. She hardly knew the man well enough to predict what he would or wouldn't do.

She peeked over the rock and looked at the machete again, at least six feet away, out in the open. Too far. The second she moved, Alejandro would pull her back.

She glanced at Mochi on her other side and caught him looking at the machete as well, pulling away from her. She tightened her hold on him. No way would she let the boy risk his life. They would wait for a better opportunity to break away.

Mochi sent her a pleading look. She gave her head a barely perceptible shake. The boy sat back on his heels, understanding the message. But a minute later he was pulling away from her again, inching toward the bushes behind him.

She was ready to stop the boy, but then noticed at last what had gotten his attention this time. A line of ants was marching along the layers and layers of dead leaves that covered the ground. The small, reddish insects moved in an endless line, one following the other.

She had no trouble recognizing them: fire ants. She'd seen them in Texas growing up, had been taught to avoid them since their stings hurt like the devil.

She knew from one of the lectures her older sisters had given her that once the first ant bit, it sent some signal to the others and they all attacked at once, en masse. She pulled as far from the line as possible without drawing Alejandro's attention. She had enough painful stings already.

Mochi silently placed a small stick in their path. After a moment of confusion and a minor pile-up, the ants crawled over it.

She glanced at Alejandro, but the man was busy scanning their surroundings for a sign of Jase, his gun ready to shoot the second he spotted his enemy.

She went back to watching Mochi from the corner of her eye, careful not to direct Alejandro's attention to him. The boy picked up the stick and gouged a line in the ground, filled it with water from his canteen. The ants didn't like the water. They went around that.

Which seemed to make the boy happy. He extended the miniature ditch all the way to Alejandro's boots. While the man stared straight forward, Mochi poured out the rest of his water, creating a handy little moat. And there the ants went, looking for a way around the water, marching toward Alejandro.

They reached his boots pretty quickly. Since that was a dry land obstacle, their tactic was to climb it. Up and up in a neat row. They couldn't get into the man's pants. He'd tucked in his pant legs as anyone who knew anything about the jungle did, but up they climbed onto his back, until they reached his collar. Then in they went, one after the other.

Mochi shot her a pleased, impish smile.

She gave him a big grin.

They waited, looking anywhere but at the man. She didn't want him to suddenly turn and catch her staring, and realize that they were up to something. An agonizing minute passed. Then suddenly Alejandro jerked and whacked his back with his free hand. And then the next second, he was jumping up and vaulting over the log, dropping his second gun so he could rip his shirt off as he swore like a bandit.

For a moment nothing else moved, and her fears that Jase had left seemed confirmed. But then he swung out of the trees on a jungle vine, knocking Alejandro off his feet, and she started to breathe again.

The two tangled in a snarl of limbs, each trying to get the upper hand. They both still had their guns, so she stayed in cover and kept Mochi with her in case one of the men got off a shot and it went wide. But Jase had Alejandro's right wrist in a firm grip, and Alejandro had Jase's. Since they couldn't use their weapons, they butted heads, kicked, elbowed and generally tried to break each other's ribs instead.

Alejandro rolled Jase over a small pile of sharp rocks that ripped his pants. And his skin, she realized a second later when she saw red spreading on the fabric. Jase barely grunted at the injury. He focused completely on his enemy as the two rolled toward the creek.

Then rolled right into the rapid water.

Jase held Alejandro's head under for a long minute, before Alejandro heaved him off and returned the favor. And kept Jase under way too long. A dark, demented smile began spreading on the man's face.

She worked herself up to her knees, fear coursing through her, quickly growing into panic. The fight between the two men would decide her fate. And Alejandro looked to be winning. She couldn't bear thinking what would happen to her, to her baby, to Mochi...

No, a determined voice bubbled up from somewhere deep inside her. *You can take control.*

For a second, she fought that voice. That she could do anything in the current situation sounded crazy. She wasn't like Jase, hadn't been trained for this, had never been in a fight in her life.

But hadn't she resolved to take charge of her life?

Then do it.

So this was a rough situation. Yes, she had a better than good chance of getting hurt. But the price of remaining passive was even greater.

She gestured to Mochi to stay put, hoping he would understand what her upheld palm meant. Then she slipped around the rock as quietly as she could with her big belly, went for the machete and hid it behind her back. She approached the men from behind.

And then she was close enough, had made it to within reach. Alejandro was too focused on Jase to notice her.

So far so good. Now what? She balked at the actual violence part of the deal.

She didn't dare use the blade. If she missed Alejandro, she could easily slice something off Jase. But she had to do something. She'd gotten this far. She was going to fight, dammit.

She lifted the weapon over her head, meaning to bring the handle down hard on the back of Alejandro's head and knock him out, except Jase had made his move at the same second and came up from the water to roll Alejandro under again.

So the butt of the machete glanced off Alejandro's cheek, and she hit Jase in the eye with all her strength. She could have easily blinded him but, thank God, the machete had a wide handle and his cheekbone took the brunt of the hit.

Alejandro roared and shoved her back, into the water, then went for Jase, but the sound of a gunshot had him whipping his head in the direction of the sound. That moment of hesitation was enough for Jase to wrest control of the situation again.

He grabbed Alejandro, going for the man's throat.

Melanie struggled to stand, but her feet kept slipping, her considerable weight pulling her back. She floundered in the middle of the creek where the water was deeper and the current swifter. Swift enough to move her.

She stifled a moan of panic, but Jase heard her anyway and looked at her.

Alejandro used the distraction and tore away from him, lurching toward the opposite bank.

She struggled for control. "I'm fine."

Jase threw himself after the man.

Then the hand she braced herself with slipped and she suddenly lost the fight. The rapid flow of water washed her downcreek. She did her best to protect her belly with her arms, cried out on instinct, without meaning to. "Jase!"

The current rolled her to the side and she swallowed some water, her ungainly body impossible to maneuver.

JASE GAVE UP on Alejandro immediately and leapt back into the water, sloshed to where she struggled with the current. He pulled her up carefully, making sure she didn't slip again, didn't hit her belly. "Are you all right? Where are you hurt?"

He looked for cuts and bruises, silently swearing at himself for not paying closer attention to her. She could have been hurt. Her baby could have been...

It was the first time he thought of the baby as a real person instead of a remote concept. A baby that might have her eyes. The thought made him feel all weird.

"He's getting away!" She pulled away from him to point at the spot where Alejandro was running for the bushes on the opposite bank. He no longer had his weapon. Must have dropped it in the water. He dove into the forest, and judging by the way the branches were moving, he didn't stop. Probably heading back to camp.

Jase grabbed his gun and aimed. Too late. The dense vegetation swallowed his target. He didn't want to squeeze the trigger blindly. He hadn't forgotten that shot in the distance earlier. Better not draw attention to himself until he knew who was out there.

He helped Melanie to shore, careful that she wouldn't slip again and hurt herself. He tried not to notice how nice it felt to have her tucked into his arms. She fit perfectly.

"So do you know if it's a boy or a girl?" he asked,

not knowing why exactly, as he tugged her toward dry ground. Her baby was none of his business.

"Boy." She smiled even as she gasped for air and braced her back, dripping wet and leaning on him. "I'm going to name him William. For my grandfather."

Not for the boy's father. Maybe her brief marriage had been... What? What was he hoping for here? That she wasn't still in love with Julio? What difference did it make to him?

Don't be stupid.

Just because he'd had a few hot dreams about her, a new one last night, and because the more time they spent together, the more he was starting to like her gentleness with Mochi and Chico and her grit of never uttering a word of complaint while other women would want to be fussed over and spoiled at this stage—

Fine. He liked her. Nothing wrong with that. For the next few days, they were in this together. They were teammates.

But then he was going to drop her off, put her from his mind and focus on the op again.

"Sorry about your eye." She looked up at him, wincing.

"Forget it," he said, but then he grinned. "We must make an odd-looking couple." Her eyes were getting better little by little, but were still plenty swollen.

"The best thing about the jungle is that it doesn't have any mirrors," she told him. Then she asked, "What was that gunshot earlier?" Apparently she hadn't forgotten, either. "Who else is out there?"

"No idea. But whoever they are, they're not our friends." He knew that for a fact because he had no friends in the jungle. He'd been dropped in on his own, on a solo mission, no team to back him up. You didn't take an entourage with you when you went undercover.

Mochi came to help, the puppy jumping around at their feet. Jase turned in the direction where the gunshot had come from, but could hear nothing else. So, as he lowered Melanie down to a fallen log, he turned his attention back to the spot where Alejandro had disappeared.

He could probably still catch up with the man. He'd always been able to outrun him.

He looked at Melanie, her tortured eyes and soggy clothes, which, oddly, detracted nothing from her beauty. She was such a lovely mess. Her eyes filled with trust as she looked at him, and that strange fluttering feeling started up in his chest again.

No time to think about that now.

He considered the distant gunshot. Someone or, most likely, a whole group of people walked the jungle not far from here. Maybe half a mile to the north. Could be poachers or illegal loggers.

Either way, he couldn't leave Melanie and Mochi to chase after Alejandro.

"I should have shot the bastard when I had the chance," he said under his breath, mostly to himself. Should have taken aim when the idiot had jumped from behind the log, ripping at his shirt. But the man was jiggling around so much, he'd been afraid that a bullet could go astray and hit either Melanie or Mochi.

He raised an eyebrow. "What did you two do to him?"

"Fire ants." Melanie grinned. "Mochi did it."

He nodded at the boy with appreciation.

"You should have shot him," she said.

"I thought about it." But even beyond not wanting to take the chance that a shot would go wide... "I was hoping to ask him a few questions first." You never shot someone without first trying to gain useful intelligence. The U.S. was desperate for information about the Don's terrorist contacts.

Which he wasn't going to get now, dammit.

He couldn't go back to camp after he'd dropped off Melanie and Mochi. They'd be waiting for him. They knew he'd taken her. He couldn't talk his way out of this one. He swore silently.

The op was speedily going to hell in a handbasket. He needed a plan B.

Melanie squeezed water from her shirt. Once again, she was soaked to the skin. They both were. "What do we do now?"

A light breeze was blowing from the north. Whoever had squeezed off that shot wouldn't smell their smoke. "We start a fire and dry our clothes a little. I want you to have a little more rest, anyway, before we get back on the trail. And we all need to eat something."

"Shouldn't we get moving? Alejandro knows where we are."

"It'll take him a while to get back to camp. And the Don can't afford to send a whole group after us just now. He'll need every man for the battle. We have some time to rest."

He started the fire, using the inside of an abandoned termite mound for kindling. He'd spotted the mound from up in the tree when he'd been preparing for his swing.

While he worked on getting the flames going, Melanie peeled off as much clothing as she could without completely stripping. He kept his gaze off her, giving her privacy. Of course, even without staring, he caught enough from his peripheral vision to get his body humming.

Even with the hornet stings and a couple of new bruises, she had a certain serenity and definite beauty about her. She had strength, although he wasn't sure she realized just how much. But she was also vulnerable. He responded to the first quality, but it was the second that seemed to draw him irresistibly.

He always wanted to protect everyone. Just didn't know when to give up, especially when it came to saving damsels in distress. This wasn't the first time his savior complex had jeopardized a mission.

He had an idea where it came from. He was the only son of a widowed mother. The last thing his father had made him promise before he'd died was that Jase would protect her. He'd been five years old. He'd grown up fantasizing about a million ways in which he would save his mom and make Dad proud in heaven.

Instead of crying when he missed his dad, because boys weren't supposed to cry, he would lose himself in those fantasies. He'd watched his father's extensive superhero movie collection a million times. Dad had been a major comic book addict.

Sometimes Jase wondered if he'd ever even had a choice other than to become a special ops soldier. Sure, he didn't have superpowers, but he had supertraining. Where else did you get to save the world on a daily basis?

He looked at the pregnant woman, the kid and the three-legged puppy, more than aware that by not going after Alejandro, he'd just ruined his mission and instead chosen the motley crew in front of him.

He rubbed a hand over his face. *Oh, man.* The colonel was going to kill him. Right after he fired him.

He shrugged out of his shirt, then hung their clothes on the branches around the fire. He handed out some venison jerky. Then he took his gun apart, dried it, put it back together. Anything to keep his mind and hands busy. After that, he repacked the backpack Melanie had stolen from him earlier. He liked things in their place. There was a science to packing for a long trek in the jungle.

"Sorry about that," she apologized again when she realized what he was doing. "I shouldn't have run away."

True, but he couldn't blame her for it. She'd thought he was one of Don Pedro's conscienceless thugs. All her actions proved was that she had good survival instincts.

She watched him. "I'm glad that you were at the right place at the right time to rescue us from Pedro. I don't think either of us would have made it without you. It's nothing short of amazing that you could get us all safely away from camp." She smiled. "I guess that's why you're the expert."

The acknowledgment felt good, especially coming from her. But he had to be careful not to let it go to his head. "I don't normally do search-and-rescue missions," he told her before she could get too carried away.

"Can you tell me what you do? If you can't, I understand."

She would. But knowing a little bit about him would probably make her feel better, safer. After what she'd been through, she deserved that. "I do about 30 percent intelligence gathering, 60 percent search-and-destroy, 10 percent wild-card ops."

"What's that?"

"Either too many unknown parameters in an op, or constantly shifting parameters. Basically, you figure out your course of action as you go." Which this deal here was rapidly turning into.

Chico hobbled over to him and he remembered the wooden peg in his pocket. He pulled it out, set it into the hole he'd cut in the chunk of leather he'd made for this purpose, then tied the thing into place over the dog's shoulders—a makeshift prosthetic leg.

Chico sat, sniffed the wood first, then chewed on it.

Jase lifted the puppy to his feet, gave him a gentle shove. And damned if Chico didn't hobble forward, then look up at him with a comically surprised look on his face.

Mochi, who'd come up to see what he was about, laughed out loud, threw himself to the ground and rolled around in glee.

Jase glanced at Melanie, who was looking at him like he was some kind of hero.

"He's going to need some practice," he said gruffly, but deep down he was just a little pleased.

Mochi immediately started training the puppy to move forward, engrossed in the task. Jase watched for a few more minutes, then busied himself with the fire.

When their clothes were semidry, at least not dripping, he handed them out. After they all got dressed, he put away Chico's peg leg—didn't want to hurt the puppy by having it on too long too soon—then led Melanie and the boy back to the path. They backtracked to their original trail that went straight north and followed that.

He kept his eyes open. Whoever had squeezed off that shot earlier could be far away by now—it was a big jungle—but still…

"Let's keep as quiet as we can," he told the others, hoping the puppy would mind his words, too.

He kept listening for any unusual, out-of-place noises. But peeling his ears didn't help much. The birds and the bugs were loud enough to drown out most everything else. There could be people ahead of them on the trail, and he wouldn't know it until they practically bumped into each other.

Since they were pushing through a thicker patch of vegetation again, visibility was maybe six feet. He marched forward quietly, all his senses alert, until they reached the area from where he thought the gunshot might have had originated.

He stopped, looking for any sign of an ambush waiting ahead. He glanced up at the tall trees around them and shot Mochi a questioning look. Mochi grinned at him, immediately understanding his meaning. As bad as his circumstances were, Mochi smiled more than anyone Jase had ever seen. He appreciated that about the kid. He was a tough little guy, for sure. He was going to be a great warrior someday.

He gave Mochi a boost up the tree and the boy took it from there. The kid could have outclimbed a monkey. He weighed practically nothing and his limbs were flexible. And he had no fear, apparently, which helped a great deal.

Jase put his gear down and stood ready to catch him should the boy slip, although he didn't expect that to happen. The boy stopped when he was about forty feet up, and looked around in every direction. Then he pointed straight ahead.

Jase signaled to him to come back down.

"How many?" he asked Mochi in Spanish, after the boy landed in the soft leaf mold, jumping from the lowest branch, and bounced back up to his feet.

"Many." Mochi puffed out his chest, apparently very proud of himself for the well-done recon mission.

Of course, *many* could mean absolutely anything. Jase had met natives who had only three counting words: *one, two* and *many*. The government didn't even attempt to educate the forest-dwelling Indians. And they sure didn't trust any fancy white man's learning, anyway. They had the skills they needed to survive. If they wanted anything from outsiders, it was to be left alone.

"This many?" Jase held up all five fingers on his right hand.

Mochi rapidly nodded, smiling wide.

"Or this many?" Jase added the fingers of the other hand.

Mochi kept nodding.

Great.

Jase gave Melanie the machete, then put his backpack back on and grabbed his gun, kept it out as he started down the path. He wanted to see what exactly they faced, so he knew how wide a berth to give the men when they went around them.

"You better fall a little behind," he told the others. "If anyone starts shooting at us, I'll return fire. You take off running and keep on running. Do you understand?"

Melanie nodded, concern on a face that was steadily improving, probably from Mochi's mushroom treatment. She glanced at the boy.

"Don't you worry about him," Jase told her. "He can keep up and then some. If I don't come right away, just watch what he eats and where he drinks. Whatever he does, you just copy him. He knows the jungle."

Not that he planned on engaging anyone in a fight. He hoped to scout out the enemy, then find a way around them.

But the more he progressed, the shakier that plan seemed. Soon he could smell the smoke from at least two dozen fires. He could hear voices. He signaled to Melanie and Mochi to pull off the trail, hide in the bushes and stay still. Then he stole forward on his own, crawling the last few yards on his stomach.

What he saw when he got close enough sobered him quickly. Their path wasn't blocked by a small group of poachers or rival drug runners or loggers. The men, way too many of them, all wore gray uniforms with the familiar red insignia on their armbands. The Republican Army. Soldiers were spread out as far as the eye could see in every direction.

He considered this new bit of intelligence carefully.

The chances of them being here at this spot at this time on a random military exercise were slim to none. Most likely, their presence had something to do with the drug wars. Either the government had gotten wind of the fight and sent the troops in to take out both Don Pedro and Cristobal in the same offensive, or one of those crime bosses had bought enough politicians to send in the troops to take out his enemy.

Either way, the jungle crawling with soldiers made everything much more difficult. At the very least, going around the troops was going to add miles to their trek, which was the dead-last thing they needed.

Chapter Eight

Melanie plodded forward, wet and miserable.

"Do you want me to carry the puppy?" she asked Mochi in a mixture of Spanish and hand gestures, but the boy shook his head.

Just as well. Her feet felt like lead. Not that the puppy would have added much weight. She liked the wiggling fur ball. She shuffled on, trying not to show how tired she was. Jase called for too many breaks on her account. If she slowed them down any more, they would never get to their destination. Bad enough that the detour would add another day to their journey.

They marched on until nightfall, which came way too fast. Then Jase set about making them a campsite to spend the night, starting with a fire. She helped as much as she could, then sat down once her back started to hurt. She patted her belly as her son shifted.

"Are you okay?" Jase asked immediately as he rummaged through his bag for their dinner.

"Baby is kicking. Let's hope he finds a more comfortable spot for himself tonight. He spent last night sitting on my kidney."

He blinked, an uncomfortable expression crossing

his face. His mouth opened, then closed as he cleared his throat, obviously unsure how to respond.

"Sorry." She flashed him an apologetic smile. "I was planning to have my girlfriends around me at this stage." She missed not being able to talk to anyone about all the things she was experiencing, not being able to compare notes.

If there was a time in a woman's life when she needed her friends around her, pregnancy was it.

"It's okay." Jase pushed the bag aside, then moved to make some herbal tea to go with their meal. "You'll be fine."

"Will we?" Suddenly she felt an overpowering need for reassurance. "This is not how I pictured it. I had plans..." She blinked back a rush of tears. Hormones brought them on at the most inopportune moments.

He left the water to boil and came over to her, took her hands. He rubbed a callused thumb over the back of her fingers. She soaked up the comforting touch, then she turned his hand over. His palm was a mess of blisters and calluses. He'd been working that machete hour after hour, every single day.

He didn't seem to notice. His full attention was focused on her. "Stress is probably the worst thing for both you and the baby at this stage. I know it's rough, but if you can, just try to roll with the punches. You made it this far. It's almost over."

He was right. She nodded.

"I know this is not what you're used to, but it's everyday business to the native tribes. Millions of women walked through endless woods like this through history, carrying their babies. And the overwhelming majority of those babies were born in good health." He gave a flat smile. "Well, that's what I tell myself, anyway, when the urge comes to freak out completely. I don't have all that much experience with this."

She smiled back and nodded. At that moment she wouldn't have traded his company for any number of girlfriends.

"I'm going to keep you safe," he said. "I'm going to make sure this turns out all right." His gaze bore into hers.

"You're good at this rescue thing, you know that? Maybe you should change specialties."

He shook his head. "Not my strength. It's better to keep a little distance when you're a professional soldier. I get too involved. I get carried away."

"You have a weakness? No way," she teased.

"It's okay to have a weak spot, as long as you're aware of it so you can work around it."

She knew all about weak spots. "I was going to save myself, for once. I was going to escape and walk to safety. I swore that I wasn't going to need anyone to take care of me again."

"How about you start that quest for complete independence when you get back home?"

"I *can* take care of myself, you know," she said, her defenses rising.

"I know you can."

Huh? Nobody had told her that before. She looked at him with some suspicion, wondering if he was just humoring her, but his expression seemed earnest.

"I don't even doubt that you could walk out of the jungle by yourself," he said after a moment. "The research station is not that far. You know the direction.

There's plenty of rainwater to drink, and a person can go days without food."

That's right. She sat up a little straighter on her log. She could.

"Add Mochi to the mix and you're as good as there. Between the two of you, you have all kinds of skills. So if anything should happen to me, I want the two of you to just keep going."

What would happen to him? Did he plan on leaving her and going back to his mission? "I don't want anything to happen to you," she blurted.

He gave a slow smile that went straight to her heart.

That infernal awareness that refused to go away blossomed between them once again.

But then Mochi asked him something, and she dropped his hands and stepped away, busying herself with getting ready for the night. He checked Mochi's arm, then went to see about the tea.

He'd set up a cozy campsite for them, the hammocks close to each other, the fire placed so the smoke wouldn't hit them but would still keep some of the insects away.

When the tea was done he unwrapped the venison jerky and the flatbread he'd set out earlier, and they had a decent meal.

The prospect of spending another night in the open didn't seem as scary as before, now that she'd survived one night like this already.

She couldn't deny the homey sense to the scene— Jase and she sitting by the fire while Mochi played with the puppy, training him with that peg leg. She caught herself smiling more than once as she watched them.

Then the boy picked up the dog, and together they settled into his hammock.

Like a family camping trip.

She'd have that someday—under normal circumstances—with her mellow music teacher. Who somehow seemed less appealing now than when she'd first invented him. She wondered where Jase would be then. Probably in a place very much like this. The thought started a dull ache inside her. She took another sip of her tea.

He went to put a few more logs on the fire. The flames behind him outlined his powerful physique, a sturdy frame with solid muscles. He was built for fighting, for this life, for dominating the environment around him and winning. He wasn't afraid of anyone or anything. Her exact opposite.

He strode back to their log when he was done and settled in, checking and cleaning his gun. They sat in companionable silence for a while.

"Let me see your stings," he said after he'd finished and put the weapon away.

He cupped her chin and turned her face toward the light of the fire, brushed her hair away with his long fingers. And there came that damned awareness again.

His touch unnerved her. She remembered their kiss back at the hacienda and she wondered if he was thinking the same, because suddenly his gaze dipped to her lips.

The night vibrated with tension around them.

"I wish we didn't have to leave camp in such a hurry and you had more time to try to seduce me," he said with a devilish grin.

Her breath caught. *Keep it lighthearted.* She pulled up a cocky eyebrow. "Try?"

He laughed.

The sound went straight to her heart. She had to do something to stop that.

"Do you flirt with all the women you rescue?" she asked.

The smile slid off his face as he pulled away.

She'd clearly hit a nerve. Should she apologize? "None of my business." His private life was his private life.

"I have this thing…" he mumbled.

She threw him a questioning look.

"Like a rescue complex or something," he confessed in a low voice. "I'm working on it."

They sat in silence for a while.

"I have the opposite problem," she said at last. "I think if someone is trying to help me it must mean that they love me. So in looking for love, I continually put myself in situations where I need to be rescued. Comes from having parents who were both too busy with their academic careers to pay any attention to me whatsoever when I was a kid, except when I was hurt."

"That's a lot of insight," he observed. "Sounds like you got your money's worth in therapy."

"All free." She gave a sour smile. "One of my best friends at work is a psychologist."

"Where do your friends think you are now?"

"Safe and sound at my wealthy brother-in-law's country estate, too far off the beaten path to be in cell phone range." Which meant nobody was calling the police to search for her. But even if some of her friends did, Pedro had the local police bought and paid for. They wouldn't go anywhere near him.

"Ironic that the one time I truly, badly need rescuing, nobody even knows I'm in trouble."

"I'm here," he said simply.

Yes, he was.

"We're not a good combination, are we? We play right into each other's misguided needs. My need to be rescued and yours to rescue." She could only imagine the dysfunctional relationship that would result if two people like them ever got together.

He shook his head.

"It can't be easy to have a normal relationship with the work you do," she observed, wondering if he felt as lonely as she did in the middle of the night.

"I thought I was in love once," he said after a few minutes, staring into the fire. "She turned out to be a counterspy and nearly killed me in the end. I survived, but my stupidity cost lives."

"Let me know if you want to talk to my shrink girl-friend someday. I'll set you up."

He gave her a flat smile.

She couldn't even imagine the kind of life he lived, a life where he couldn't trust anyone, not even the woman he was falling in love with.

Then again, a little mistrust might be healthy. In hindsight, she'd trusted Julio way too fast, married him even faster. She should have waited until she knew something about his family. That would have saved her a lot of grief, for sure.

She watched as Jase fed the flames. "Do you miss your family when you're on a mission?"

He looked back at her. "My parents are gone. Never

had any brothers and sisters. The type of work I do is best suited for men without close family ties."

That sounded terribly lonely. She wasn't sure what to say.

"You?"

"My mother and father passed away, but I have two older sisters in the States. They were both out of the house by the time I was growing up." Didn't believe a word about the neglect she'd lived through, that their parents had simply run out of attention and patience by the time she was born.

She'd worn clothes for years after they were too small, had to fend for herself pretty much as far as food went. Her parents ate at the university cafeteria, so her mother rarely remembered to cook at home. About the only time they seemed to realize that she was alive was when she was sick or hurt. She'd learned to use that.

Then she'd learned, once she'd grown up, that she needed to stop such self-defeating habits. She wasn't mad at her parents. They'd been who they had been.

"I don't have a lot of warm and fuzzy memories of my childhood, and I'm unwilling to pretend for my sisters' sake that I do, which causes friction," she admitted, aware of his nearness, of his full attention on her, his graphite eyes watching her solemnly.

Her father had gotten even stranger after her mother's death. Flipped over to supercontrolling. He couldn't prevent the death of his beloved wife but, by God, he was going to protect his accident-prone daughter now. From everything. Trouble was, she was in college by then.

Ignored when she'd needed care. Practically locked up when she should have been trying her wings.

Compared to her, Jase seemed amazingly pulled to-gether. He smelled woodsy and manly, a tantalizing scent that seeped inside her and messed with her senses, so she prattled on to prove that she was unaffected.

"My sisters resent my version of the past, so now we have this gap between us. I'm going to end that non-sense as soon as I get home. They're going to be Wil-liam's aunts. The time I spent at the camp as Pedro's prisoner put a lot of things into perspective."

Longing unfurled deep inside her. "I miss my sis-ters."

She'd been working on her Ph.D. in South America for so long, she was used to not seeing them a lot. But all of a sudden she wanted them desperately, wanted to stay alive to see them again. Tears sprung to her eyes. She wiped them away. Stupid pregnancy hormones again.

When the next batch of tears came, Jase brushed them away with the pad of his thumb. And then he leaned in and kissed her.

Any thoughts of loneliness were shoved to the back of her mind as his warm lips settled over hers.

Her nerves didn't get the better of her like the first time. He was no longer a stranger. He was no longer a bandit. He was the man who'd saved her life on more than one occasion, the man who'd saved an orphaned kid and a three-legged puppy. He was the man who was going to lead all of them out of the jungle.

She liked the way he kissed: not like some starved wild man, not manhandling her, but holding her and kissing her gently, letting her set the pace. It lulled her into feeling safe with him, and because she felt safe, she could truly enjoy the kiss.

Pleasure bloomed in her body, spreading through

her, making her lose herself in the moment and in his kiss. When she pulled back after a long, titillating minute, he didn't try to hold her back. He just looked at her with a dazed expression on his face.

He cleared his throat. "We'd better get some sleep."

An image of the two of them in a proper bed, together, flashed into her mind, and heat spread through her in a flash. She found the picture irresistibly appealing. She'd been alone for months and months now, isolated at the compound. He was the first person she could trust. Falling for him would have been so incredibly easy.

And so beyond-belief stupid.

He was going to leave her in a few days. They were never going to see each other again.

She pushed up to a standing position and waddled to her hammock without looking back at him.

HE NEEDED TO stop kissing her.

The lingering taste of her on his lips was damn distracting.

Despite what she thought of him, he didn't make a habit of having affairs with women he saved. Just the one. And that had turned out disastrously.

Letting his testosterone run away with him where Melanie was concerned had the potential of ending even worse. She was pregnant. There was a baby to be considered. Having a child alone had to be difficult enough. He didn't want to step into the middle of all that and mess up her life even worse.

Even if he wanted her, child and all.

Crazy.

He'd never seen himself as a father figure. He liked

saving people, the adventure of it, but the long-term taking care of them… He wasn't sure how good he'd be at that. His job didn't exactly spell family man.

He settled into his hammock, his body hard as a rock. "I don't know where that came from. Sorry about the kiss," he called over.

"Don't ever apologize for a kiss like that," she called back after a second, quoting him.

He grinned into the darkness.

He really liked her.

"How much farther is it to the research station?" she asked after a little while.

"Two more days." Too long, and in a way not nearly long enough. "We're about halfway there. You handled everything fine so far. You'll handle the rest just the same. Piece of cake."

HE REMEMBERED THAT sentiment two days later and wished he'd never tempted fate by saying it. Jase swore silently as he stepped into the large clearing and took in the charred, empty building where a fully staffed research station should have been.

The outpost had been attacked and burned—a few days before, from the look of it. He signaled to Melanie and Mochi to stay back, stay in the cover of the palm trees.

"Hello," he called out as he moved forward, then stepped into the building, his gun ready.

No response came.

He saw a number of rust-colored stains on the wall as he walked, then more dried blood on the floor in one of the bedrooms. But he found no bodies as he cleared the station room by room.

He checked the kitchen for supplies, since he didn't have much left in his backpack. But whoever had ransacked the place had cleared out pretty much everything. He searched for the station's radio equipment, but what hadn't been ripped out had been bashed to pieces.

He wished, not for the first time, that he still had his own phone. The research station had a patch cleared for a landing helicopter. He could call in his location and they'd have a rescue team here within hours.

Disappointment washed through him as he moved to one of the windows and waved to Melanie and Mochi to let them know that it was safe to come in.

"What happened to the people?" She looked around wide-eyed and a little green around the gills when they caught up with him in the central hallway.

"The staff probably called for help when the attack began. Help got here at one point and evacuated the survivors and the bodies."

She braced her back and nodded numbly. "Why would anyone attack peaceful scientists? Who would do this?"

"Either Cristobal's men or the government troops. My money is on the latter. Not all the generals are crazy about foreign presence in their country. Some consider the scientific and human aid groups coming here American spies."

A stricken expression clouded her already drawn face.

"We'll spend the day here." While the charred wood around them smelled like smoke, the fire had burned out. "You need rest."

Tension drew his shoulders tight. She was eight months pregnant. She needed to be evacuated. Now.

She nudged some broken equipment on the floor with her toe. "Do you think the people who worked here will come back?"

"Not anytime soon." Maybe not ever.

He put a hand under her elbow and helped her over to the nearest chair. She sat carefully, and when Chico ran over to her and jumped on her leg, she pulled the puppy onto her lap, ran her fingers through its soft fur. She looked tired and discouraged but thoughtful, nowhere near ready to give up. He could almost see the wheels turning in her head as she sat there, trying to come up with a plan.

He was doing the same, cataloging everything he saw, trying to figure out what might be useful to them.

"How about the Jesuit mission?" she asked after a few minutes.

That stopped him in his tracks. "What Jesuit mission?"

"A couple of weeks ago, Consuela got word that her oldest son, the drug runner, got sick in prison. She took a few days to walk to the Jesuit mission to have prayers said for him."

A place like that within walking distance to camp... Why hadn't he heard of it? Then again, the men weren't the churchgoing kind. "Are you sure?"

"As far as I know, it's farther from camp than this place, but it's definitely there. I think one of Don Pedro's underlings had a camp that was built on the ruins of an old Jesuit mission. The army took it out recently. It was a big deal on the news. I heard it on the radio. The church stepped up and decided to take the place back and minister to the natives."

Sounded like a PR opportunity nobody could resist.

But he didn't care whether the army had acted because they were genuinely interested in stamping out the drug trade, or because Cristobal had bought a small unit to take care of his rivals for him.

If the mission had been a camp in the not-too-distant past, that meant it was near one of the jungle roads. The drugs were usually distributed by old army jeeps, except in the most remote areas where the men still used mules.

But a Jesuit mission… Sounded like an important place. It would have a road for sure, and vehicles, very likely.

He grinned wide as something suddenly occurred to him. "I think I know exactly where that mission is."

He had the GPS coordinates from Mitch Mendoza, an SDDU operative. Mitch had been sent into the jungle last year to rescue someone from one of Don Pedro's underlings, a guy called Juarez who'd since disappeared. The camp Mitch had described had been built on the ruins of an old mission. It had to be one and the same.

The SDDU had gained a lot of usable intel on that op. In fact, Jase's current mission was a direct result of what Mitch had started. He wished he had Mitch here right now, but since the man had been known around these parts in the past, he worked the op from another angle now with his new wife—no slouch herself, ex-CIA. They were undercover on the Mexican side of the U.S. border, keeping tabs on the human trafficking business.

Jase grabbed a pen from the floor, then picked through the hundreds of printouts and charts that had been tossed around until he found a torn map. He laid it on a desk and did his best to mark it up, using his few points of reference.

Melanie leaned over to watch.

"We're about here." He drew a big X. "This is Don Pedro's camp." He marked that with a square. "Cristobal's men are probably still there, fighting. The army troops we ran into are about here." He closed his eyes and brought up a picture of Roberto's satellite map in his head and Mitch's coordinates. "The mission should be somewhere around here." He marked the spot with the sign of the cross.

"How far?"

"At least another day's walk. But it's a straight shot, nowhere near that army unit, so we don't have to worry about them."

But time was not the only issue. She was as tough as anyone he'd ever met. Still, she couldn't be pushed endlessly. He rubbed his hand over his face.

"But?" she asked, picking up on his change of mood.

"We have no more food. We have to hunt as we go." And that would slow them down.

"You said a person can go for days without food."

"In an absolute emergency. But (A), you're pregnant, and (B), the weaker we get the slower we'll be able to go. It wouldn't make any sense starving ourselves on purpose. It's a lot easier to hang on without food for a day or two when you're holed up somewhere. Marching on an empty stomach is a lot more difficult."

He kept an eye on Mochi, who was examining the research station wide-eyed, looking at machines he'd never seen in his life. Just the building must have seemed like magic to him, a sprawling unit of wood and Plexiglas, twice the size of Don Pedro's hacienda and probably twenty times bigger than the largest dwelling had been in the boy's village.

He seemed excited and impressed at this strange

place in the middle of the jungle. He didn't seem scared of any of it, just curious, conversing with the puppy rapidly in his native language.

"Can you hunt around here before we head out?" Melanie asked.

"I'll try. But keep in mind that there was a fairly big fight here recently. Then the rescue chopper coming and going. Fire, too, at one point. The smell of charred wood is still in the air. Game might avoid the surrounding area for a couple of days."

She looked grim at that assessment.

And he wished he'd kept his mouth shut. The last thing he'd wanted to do was discourage her.

"How about this? You go and get some rest in one of the bedrooms, in a real bed, and I'll go look around. If there's game anywhere nearby, I'll bring it back. That's a promise."

She brightened. "They have real beds here?"

"You bet."

She slid off the chair. Hesitated. "Can I do anything to help?"

He couldn't do anything but smile. "You're doing good. With the independence thing. Here you are, eight months pregnant and offering to follow me into the jungle to look for game. That's pretty self-reliant."

Her eyes went wide with unspoken pleasure, the corners of her mouth turning up. "You think?"

"You bet. You're so independent you barely even set off my protective instincts anymore."

"Really?"

He looked at her and fought the urge to pick her up and hand-carry her out of the jungle. "Okay, I might still feel a little protective. But that's my fault, not yours," he assured her. Then he turned to Mochi and told him in Spanish to stay and guard the *señora,* a task that seemed to please the boy to no end.

Jase left the old pistol with them. Not because he thought Melanie would need it, but to increase her sense of security. The building smelled like smoke and humans. That should keep the wild animals at bay. She and the boy should be perfectly safe. Yet Jase found himself reluctant to leave them as he walked away.

And, not for the first time, he had a feeling that his protective feelings toward her might not come from his usual must-save-all complex, that there was something else between them, some sort of a link he couldn't name. He shook off that weird notion and headed off into the forest for some bush meat.

"IT's A SNAKE, isn't it?" Melanie looked at the chunks of white meat that had been carefully cleaned and chopped and could have easily passed for chicken, except she knew better.

Jase fired up the propane stove, one of the very few things that had miraculously escaped damage. He'd brought the meat neatly wrapped in a banana leaf, but dumped it into a proper skillet now that they'd found one in all this mess. "Constrictors are perfectly safe to eat. And they're tasty." He gave her a patent used-car-salesman smile, smarmy and fake. "Honestly."

And made her laugh, which, under the circumstances, was a miracle.

She stirred the meat while he hunted for spices in the ransacked cabinets, came back with a jar of steak sauce and sprinkled some into the skillet.

She drew a deep breath. Her stomach wasn't as

queasy as it had been in her first trimester, but the pregnancy hormones did still affect it. She wasn't sure how she was going to handle this. "I've never had snake before."

He gave her a patient look. "Of course you have. What do you think bush meat is?"

The women made bush meat stew a lot. The menu at camp contained little else, in fact, except when they had someone coming in for a meeting from a bigger town nearby and they brought a side of beef, but that only happened once a month maybe, or less.

"Bush meat is deer," she said with confidence. "Rabbits at the very worst."

"Bush meat is whatever the men find in the bush. Monkeys, snakes, frogs, anything with meat on it."

She pressed a hand against her stomach, which gave a sudden roll. "Stop. Please." She drew a deep breath to steady herself, but that might have been a mistake.

As the meat began to fry, its aroma filled the small galley kitchen. But no, okay, she had to admit, the contents of the skillet just smelled like frying meat. She steeled her spine. Fine. A stupid chunk of meat wasn't going to defeat her. She needed the nutrition to get out of here and take her baby back home safely.

She would do whatever it took. "Okay."

He smiled at her. "See that? You're tougher than you think."

She could get used to him telling her that, she decided as he served her a plate. He handed another one to Mochi, who fell on the meat and gobbled it up. Chico didn't even chew, just inhaled everything.

She drew another deep breath. If they could do it, so could she.

"Don't look at it," Jase advised, sitting across the table, which he'd cleaned off and propped up to make up for the broken leg. "Look into my eyes and think of something else."

She put the first piece into her mouth and held his gaze. He gave her an encouraging smile. "So what's your favorite food?"

"South American cuisine. Got used to it in Rio. Julio was a fantastic cook. He really did well with that restaurant," she said as she chewed carefully. If only everything else in their life had gone as smoothly.

He'd been handsome and hot-blooded, gave her 100 percent of his attention. She'd soaked that right up. But once they were married he had that project in the bag, so to speak, and moved on to the next: opening a second restaurant. And gave his full attention to that.

He'd also become a lot more authoritative. He'd even demanded that she give up her work. Not that she had ruled that out, once the baby was born, or even had time to think about it at that point. She would just have liked to be the one to make that decision.

"I'm a steak guy, myself," Jase was telling her.

She refocused on him. "Protein is supposed to be healthy." It sure built muscles, of which he had plenty. He could have been some beef company's spokesperson.

He shrugged. "Most of the time I'm off on some mission, existing on MREs."

"MR what?"

"Meal, Ready-to-Eat. Government-issued military food. Freeze-dried, nasty stuff you have to reconstitute with water before you can eat. Doesn't have much of a taste."

He glanced over at Mochi and Chico. They were

both already done, eyeing the leftovers in the skillet. Jase divided it between them.

He hadn't touched his food yet; he was too busy distracting her.

It worked. Before she knew it, she cleared her plate, and she felt comfortably full. She needed that protein, both for herself and for William.

The baby seemed to appreciate it, too, because he started kicking. Mochi stared at her belly where he could see the movement even through her clothes. He laughed and ran to put his hand on the spot, nodding like crazy.

She glanced up at Jase, amused, but caught such a look of longing in his gaze that it made her look away.

He finished his meal while she went to the bathroom—some sort of a composting toilet—then they gathered up their belongings and started out in the direction of the rebuilt Jesuit mission, looking for an animal trail that went in that direction, to make things easier.

"Are you sure the scientists won't be coming back?" She'd counted on this place. And even if it was missing some walls and most of the roof, it still provided more protection than the jungle.

"Very unlikely. But we'll make it to the mission. It's not that much farther."

He was right, of course, so she followed him. They found a faint trail after a while and settled into a comfortable but productive pace.

They stopped regularly, and were looking for a spot to spend the night when they reached an area that had been logged in the past couple of years. With no tall trees to block the sun, the undergrowth grew especially dense, visibility reduced to no more than a couple of feet.

Heat and humidity pressed down on them. She felt as if she was surrounded by green walls in a small space, an uncomfortable, claustrophobic sensation. You couldn't see any distance, had no idea what waited for you beyond the next few steps.

Mochi prattled on about something to the dog.

She didn't understand a single word, but she liked looking at him. He was comfortable in the jungle, and the way he handled the trek, as if it was no big deal, helped her to relax a little, helped her to remember that countless people lived here and survived the forest every single day.

Jase would signal the boy to be quiet every once in a while, and he'd fall silent for a few minutes, but then he would start up the chatter again, breaking out in laughter now and then. Presumably he'd said something funny. He and the puppy were having a grand old time together, taking walking lessons with the peg leg at every stop, talking up a storm in between.

Then Jase slowed at the head of the line. He lifted his hand again for silence. Even as Mochi quieted, Chico started barking at the bushes. Mochi quickly held the dog's muzzle shut, shooting an apologetic look to Jase.

Too late.

A metallic click came from their right.

She held her breath. Maybe it wasn't a gun. Could be she heard wrong, and nothing more had happened than a branch snapping under the weight of a snake.

Mochi held the dog tighter. She pulled the kid closer to her and held her arms protectively around him.

Then Jase signaled to them to get down and aimed

his gun in the direction of the sound at the same time. But another click came from behind them, and another from ahead, then another and another.

Definitely guns being cocked.

They were surrounded by an unseen enemy.

Chapter Nine

Jase waited, every muscle in his body drawn tight.

"Put the gun down," someone shouted at him in Spanish.

Shooting had been out of the question from the start, anyway. No way would he start a gunfight with Melanie and Mochi in the middle of it. This was exactly why the average commando soldier didn't take his wife and kid into battle with him, he thought. Not that Melanie and Mochi belonged to him, but still.

If he'd been alone, he would have had half a dozen options how to play this. In the current situation… He gritted his teeth as frustration swept through him.

As he lowered his weapon the men stepped forward, one after the other, their machine guns trained on him. He counted a dozen uniformed guys, a small army unit.

"Who are you?" Their leader yanked Jase's weapon from him.

Since he was dressed in camouflage, holding a machine gun better than theirs, Jase couldn't exactly claim to be a tourist.

He reached out a hand to Melanie, who'd crouched when he'd told her to get down, and pulled her up. Squatting like that with the extra weight couldn't have been easy on her knees. None of this could be easy on her, in fact, but she was holding up admirably.

Instead of hiding behind her, Mochi stepped in front of her in a defensive move. The kid was really something.

Jase flashed him an approving look, then returned his attention to the men. He had a feeling the army was in this part of the jungle on either Don Pedro's request or Cristobal's. His fate would depend on guessing the right man. Don Pedro was the bigger boss. He was more likely to have the money to buy off a general.

"I'm taking this woman to Don Pedro," he told the man.

"You're in luck, amigo." The man gave a dark, gap-toothed grin. "That's exactly where we're going. You'll come with us."

"*Gracias,* but we'd just slow you down. You better go without us if you're in a hurry."

"Always have time for friends of the Don."

An offer of protection was a big thing in the jungle. The man would have become suspicious if they showed reluctance to accept help. Jase tried to look happy.

He ran through all the options in his head, all the ways this could play out. He distinctly hated some of the possible endings.

But they should be safe for the night, at least, he thought. Then they would have to break away at one point the next day, escape the men and head to the mission.

They could never outrun the soldiers if they were pursued. Which meant that he'd have to get his weapon back and kill the dozen men. Without Melanie and Mochi getting hurt in the process. He tallied up his ammunition. *Plenty.* He had made sure to prepare for the trip before he'd left the camp.

"What's with the kid?" The man gave Mochi a speculative look.

"Bought him off some loggers we came across. Needed a guide," Jase said, then nodded toward Melanie. "We were about to stop. She needs rest. She's the Don's sister-in-law."

"What is she doing here?"

No choice now but to lie all the way through. "They're expecting trouble at camp. I was supposed to take her to safety." He named the nearest town he knew of in the direction from which they were coming. "But my jeep busted an axle on the logging road we were taking. I have to walk her back to the Don. Figured we better take a shortcut. Still, damn slow going." He made sure to sound put-out and annoyed as if he hated getting stuck with the task.

The man's eyes narrowed, but he nodded after a few seconds. "We'll stop for the day at the next clearing we come across. She can rest there until morning."

He led the way, gesturing them to follow. Jase did just that, and then so did Melanie and Mochi. The rest of the men fell in line behind them, with the exception of two who ran ahead with machetes to clear their path. And there they went, marching down the trail again.

They didn't have to go far before they found a suitable place near a creek. Jase helped make camp, assessing each men's strengths and weaknesses. The soldiers were irritable, tired of the march and bored. He made sure to keep Melanie and Mochi as far away from them as possible. He didn't want the men to start picking on them for entertainment.

Since he had time, he built a sleeping platform instead of simply hanging their hammocks. He figured Melanie's back could use a nice flat surface to rest for a change. They washed, ate and drank. He pretended to pay attention to that, but kept an eye on the men and the sole sentry they set.

Obviously they felt safe and comfortable. And with reason. The rest of their army buddies weren't that far off, camping less than fifteen miles from here. At this point, they were definitely the strongest force in the jungle.

Their relaxed mood might just play into his hands, Jase thought as he went about his business.

When they called for Mochi, he didn't interfere, but he stood ready. Thankfully, all they wanted was the boy to climb a tree and fetch some fruit. They kept him close by so they could play with the dog, until the kid fell asleep by the fire.

Since Chico curled up right next to him, Jase let the boy stay where he was. The dog would bark if a snake came their way in the night. And if Jase showed too much affection for the kid, or acted protective, it would make the others suspicious.

So he ended up sharing the sleeping platform with only Melanie. He draped their mosquito netting around it and tucked in the edges. The camp soon quieted, everyone but the sentry settled in for sleep.

"I'm sorry," Melanie whispered next to him. "Pedro was my problem. I shouldn't have involved you in any with this."

"Hey, it ain't over till the fat lady sings," he said absentmindedly, his mind on his escape plans, then winced when he realized she might take that the wrong way. *Way to go, Campbell. Smooth all the way.*

But she patted her belly without taking offense. "I think that'd be me. I have to warn you, I can't carry a tune for anything."

That she could keep a sense of humor under the circumstances was nothing short of amazing.

Being in the same "bed" an arm's reach from her didn't exactly facilitate sleep. He tried anyway. The camp was quiet; only the bugs droned on in the trees. He looked over at her after a couple of minutes passed. Her eyes were still open.

"I'm too nervous to sleep," she admitted.

"We'll be fine."

"Is every mission like this for you? One calamity after the other?"

"Pretty much. Believe it or not, I usually like it." He lived for a good challenge. Not that his job was a game to him, but still something close; obstacles to conquer, to try himself, to prove himself, to win.

Except this time he felt none of the rush. This time the stakes had somehow changed. Melanie wasn't simply another damsel in distress. Melanie was somebody to him.

Oh, hell. That was just a whole new level of stupid, even for him. He squeezed his eyes shut for a second, as if blocking out the sight of her might solve that problem. It didn't.

"Do you think we'll ever get out of the jungle?" she asked in a whisper.

"Don't think too far ahead. Just think of right now, right here. Keep it manageable. This is all we have to deal with at the moment. Right now, right here, all we have to do is get some sleep."

"I'm scared right now, right here."

Her admission made him want to draw her into his arms, so he tried a different tactic. "I'm not taking that as a compliment," he said with feigned indignation. "I'm here protecting you. If you're still scared, that must mean you don't think I can handle it."

"Not what I meant," she said immediately.

"Well, if you think I *can* handle it, then there's nothing to be scared of."

"Is that some kind of manly logic?"

"You got something against that?"

"Hormones and feelings."

He felt his lips curve into a grin. "Now that scares me more than these jokers here."

She smiled at him through the darkness. Then she closed her eyes at last.

He watched her for a long minute, then looked behind her to examine the campsite, all without turning his head. He didn't want them to catch him spying. The sentry walked the perimeter, then sat down by the fire. Jase's weapon was there, too. They hadn't given it back to him, no matter how close to Don Pedro he'd claimed to be. He would just have to take it back on his own.

He thought of the killing that was to come, planned for various contingencies. The violence didn't bother him, although he would have preferred to avoid it if possible.

There were always options.

If he sneaked away now with Melanie, maybe their absence wouldn't be discovered until morning. Maybe they could gain enough distance. Maybe the men wouldn't bother coming after them. Who knew, they might have orders to reach the Don quickly.

Jase looked at her silhouette. He might be able to save her and her baby. But he would have to leave Mochi behind.

Then he realized that her eyes were open again and she was watching him.

"I don't want to leave the boy," he told her. The scrawny little thing was beginning to grow on him. There really was something about that kid. He knew grown men with less grit and a hell of a worse attitude about life.

"I wouldn't go without Mochi," she said without hesitation.

"Yeah. I pretty much figured."

They lay next to each other in silence.

She shifted to her side.

"Are you okay?"

"The baby is kicking up a storm. Feels like there's a soccer practice going on in there."

That must be weird as anything. He couldn't even imagine it. He'd envied Mochi earlier at the research station for being able to just walk up to her and touch her, put his hands on her belly.

But even as he thought that, Melanie reached for his hand and put it near her bellybutton that protruded through her shirt. Something pushed against his palm.

Okay. Wow.

An instant connection blinked to life. The baby just made physical contact with him.

And it was his responsibility to make sure Melanie was safe and that kid got born. The thought hit him suddenly and made him more nervous than he'd ever been on any mission before. Rescue missions were the pits, he decided. Plain nerve-wracking. He'd been smart to avoid them in the past. Search-and-destroy was a hell of a lot more straightforward.

He glanced at the men. Right. There'd be plenty of "destroy" coming his way shortly.

"You're going to be fine." This time he said the words more to reassure himself than her as he pulled his hand away, because touching her like this wasn't enough suddenly. He wanted to pull her into his arms.

"I know. I trust you."

Some warm emotion washed over him that felt kind of squishy. He didn't like it. He felt as if there was a dragnet somewhere out there, closing in around him.

"Get some rest," he told her brusquely.

And soon she did fall asleep. He watched her for a while, wondered what it would be like to sleep next to her every night. Be there when the baby was born. Get up for midnight feedings or whatever new parents tended to complain about.

Strangely, he had no problem forming a crystal-clear picture, even though he'd never seriously considered a life like that before. His focus had firmly been on other things. Like his training and his missions.

He'd never wanted anything else. Sure, he liked the action and a good rescue if he happened to be in a position to help someone, but he was always ready, even eager, to move on once the op was over. Yet he was already wondering what Melanie would be doing once she was safely back home, what her son would be like, if the kid would end up looking like her, and other idiotically stupid things.

Of course, when he fell asleep, he had another one

of those hot and heavy dreams about her, like he had every night since he'd first seen her on the balcony. He was nowhere near ready to leave that dream world when the soldiers' shouting woke him.

He came wide awake in an instant, then was out of their shelter and on his feet, yanking on his boots, which he'd hung upside down on sticks skewered into the ground to keep the bugs out.

The men were visibly angry, looking for something.

Then he put together enough snatched words. Mochi was missing.

Amazingly, Melanie slept on despite the commotion. He let her and went to investigate, scanning the camp and the surrounding bushes, more than a little worried.

"Where is he?" the leader demanded as soon as he saw Jase.

"No idea. He slept here by the fire." He looked around at the soldiers, examining each face one by one, but none of them looked guilty. They all looked as if they could have used some more sleep. More than one flashed him an annoyed look. The kid belonged to him, so any disturbance the boy caused they blamed on Jase.

"The little bastard probably ran away." He did his best to sound annoyed, like he would if he'd paid good money for a guide who'd just taken off on him.

The man gave him a hard look.

A tense moment passed between them, Jase ready for pretty much anything. He might not have had his gun but he still had his knife in his boot, and he knew how to use it. But then the guy shrugged and turned from him to yell out orders to get packing and moving as soon as everyone was ready.

He had his own marching orders, was obviously on

some kind of mission. He wasn't going to waste time with chasing after a jungle kid who meant nothing to him.

Jase grabbed some coffee, and as he walked back to Melanie he passed by his gun but didn't pick it up. The team leader was still keeping too close an eye on him.

"Mochi ran away," he said when he reached her.

She was sitting up in their little nest, combing through her hair with her fingers, watching the men. Her forehead wrinkled with worry at the news.

"He took Chico with him." He hoped the kid had stolen some food, too, but knew he probably hadn't. He seemed to prefer whatever the forest provided. At least he knew how to fend for himself. He definitely wouldn't starve to death.

She paled. "Can we find them? Are they going to be okay?"

"Maybe Mochi recognized something when we set camp. Maybe he knows of a village around here."

The native tribes often walked long distances in search of fruit and game, and they took their children with them on these trips so they would learn the trails that led through the jungle, would learn the locations of certain fruit trees and creeks. Mochi might have passed this way before and had remembered the way to a village he was familiar with.

He helped Melanie off the platform and offered her some coffee.

"No thanks. I quit when I found out I was pregnant." She pulled out her canteen instead and took a long drink of water. "Are you sure Mochi is going to be okay on his own?"

"Reasonably sure."

"Is there any way we could go after him?"

He'd considered that already. He shook his head, annoyed that he couldn't do more. "We have no idea when he left. And we don't know in which direction he is headed."

Her shoulders slumped as she struggled to accept that. "How long before we make our move?" she whispered after a long minute.

Despite his own worries about the boy, he smiled. She was beginning to sound like a true adventurer. "At the first opportunity."

"Are you sure about Mochi? Once we break free—"

"A lost hiker, I could track. I could even track a soldier. But forget about tracking natives, especially a kid who weighs nothing and wouldn't leave marks behind him."

He was a sharp little boy, agile and industrious. He had to trust that the kid knew what he was doing, no matter how much it went against his instincts.

One of the men trotted over with a metal bowl and tossed it onto their sleeping platform, then walked away.

"*Gracias,* amigo," Jase called after him, making a point to be cordial.

The soldiers had cooked tapioca for breakfast. He pulled the bowl closer, set it between them. But they didn't spend much time on their meal or with their morning toiletries. They were all on the trail in about twenty minutes.

He stayed close to Melanie. Then, after an hour or so, when she looked like she was tiring, he asked the men to stop. They did. They understood that she was an asset, and they wanted to make sure she reached the Don in good shape.

He watched them closely, but they didn't seem to pay him or the pregnant woman too much attention. They looked sullen. They didn't appreciate being ordered out of their comfortable garrison and being sent on a trek through the jungle.

They talked amongst each other, smoked. One broke into a whistle now and again. They seemed less than fully alert, apparently expecting no trouble. They didn't seem too wary of the jungle, either, trusting that the size of the group and the noise they made would scare off any predators.

"Next time we stop," he whispered to Melanie once they were walking again, "you ask to go relieve yourself. Just keep walking. When you can't walk any farther, hide. I'll come and get you after I deal with them."

He thought of the knife hidden in his boot. He would play the concerned escort, suggesting that maybe she'd passed out or something, giving the men no reason to mistrust him, so he could pick them off one by one as they searched for her. Then once he had his gun back, he shouldn't have too much trouble finishing off whoever was left.

He flashed her a reassuring smile, but it didn't erase the worried expression from her face.

He raised his eyebrows. "You wouldn't be doubting my superb fighting capabilities again, would you?" He puffed his chest out.

She did seem to relax a little at his light tone, and rolled her eyes. "Never."

Good.

They kept walking, keeping the pace, careful not to draw any attention to themselves.

The next section of the trail turned out to be relatively easy, so the team leader didn't call for a break until another hour had passed. As planned, Melanie asked and received permission to walk into the bushes.

But she came right back in a couple of minutes, pale and anguished.

"What is it?" Jase rushed up to her.

"I'm spotting," she said under her breath, her eyes wide with fear.

What in hell did that mean? He shot her a questioning look.

"There is blood," she whispered. "Maybe there's something wrong with the baby."

A sudden cold spread through him, despite the heat that surrounded them. He reached to brace her elbow on instinct. "Are you in pain?"

She shook her head.

"Sit." He helped her, then went to talk to the leader. "She's having trouble. There's a Jesuit mission not far from here. She needs help. We have to make a stretcher and carry her there."

"We're going to Don Pedro's camp."

"If anything happens to her and the kid, Don Pedro will have your head on a plate," Jase threatened, hot anger coursing through him as he stepped forward, coming nose to nose with the man.

But the guy didn't seem threatened. And the next second Jase found out why. A half-dozen bandits came into view on the trail, heading toward them from the direction of the Don's camp. They greeted the soldiers like old friends.

They weren't Don Pedro's men. Jase didn't recognize a single one. Which could only mean one thing.

"You work for Cristobal?" he confronted the leader, dread stiffening his spine.

The man shrugged. "You go where you get the best pay."

How in hell did Cristobal have more money than Don Pedro? A question for another day.

He held his hands up in a defensive, submissive gesture. "Look, she has nothing to do with whatever power struggle is going on. She's just a woman, trying to have her baby. Let me take her to the mission. She's nothing but a complication to you, anyway."

But the hard look on the man's face didn't change at Jase's entreaty. "If she's important to Don Pedro, then she could be useful to Cristobal. I'm thinking she's worth something, eh?"

"She needs help!" He charged at the man, but others pulled him back and shoved him aside.

And, despite the rage that pumped through him, he walked away. He needed to keep a cool head, dammit. If he got shot, then she wouldn't have anybody to protect her. He did his best to walk off his fury as he strode back to her.

"How do you feel?"

"Worried."

"Pain?"

"None. Thank God. Who are those people?" She nodded toward the newcomers.

He sat down next to her and explained the developments, his jaw still clenched.

Dismay filled her big brown eyes, which had fully recovered from the hornet stings. "But the soldiers said they were here to help Don Pedro."

"Not really. They said they were going to Don Pedro,

which isn't the same thing. This way we went with them willingly and didn't put up a fight." The leader had simply done whatever was easiest for him. He wasn't as stupid as he looked. Go figure.

He watched the men. The leader was looking at him and Melanie, explaining something to Cristobal's lackeys. Then he called out to two of his own soldiers and ordered a stretcher made.

All right. Good. The guy was smart enough to know that she was worth more alive than dead.

"What will Cristobal do with us?" she asked, a hand on her belly in that protective gesture he'd seen so often.

"Depends on how well the battle is going. If he still hasn't taken the compound, he might use you as a bargaining chip."

"And if he did?"

"We'll figure something out."

Not that he could think of a single thing just now that might save them. If Cristobal had already taken the compound, then he had no need for them. Most likely, they'd be summarily executed.

Not that he was about to share that with her.

"You know what they say," he said instead, keeping his tone light.

"It ain't over till the fat lady sings?"

Her spunk had to be appreciated.

"My lips are sealed." She straightened her spine, putting a look of determination on her face.

"That's my girl." He made sure the smile he gave her was reassuring and full of confidence.

Chapter Ten

They'd been closer to the camp than she'd thought, and the trip went faster with her on the stretcher and not slowing everyone down. They reached Cristobal's troops midafternoon, by the river. He was too busy to pay much attention to them, directing the ongoing offensive, so his lackeys settled her and Jase in until the man had time to decide their fate.

Melanie lay on a platform under a makeshift roof of bamboo and banana leaves, close enough to the battle to hear the gunfire but far enough away to be safe. Cristobal's command tent stood to her right, the man coming and going, a permanent scowl on his scarred face. He had cold, cruel eyes and a crooked nose that had obviously been broken in the past and never set straight.

The heavyset drug boss didn't look like a man given to vanity. He looked power-hungry and ruthless, ordering his men around with the self-confidence of a third-world dictator. He also looked frustrated, and ready to blame anyone and everyone for the protracted battle.

Other than worry about her baby, Melanie could do little else but observe everything around her and speculate.

Cristobal hadn't been able to take the compound in

five days. But things were looking up for him now. His army backup should be here soon. They hadn't been that far off when she and Jase had sneaked around them. Odd that they weren't here already. Seemed that they were marching awfully slowly if they covered less ground than a pregnant woman.

Maybe the general Cristobal had bought was hoping the two factions would kill each other before he got here, then he could just gather up the loot and get through all this the easy way.

She wished she could ask Jase what he thought, but he was tethered to a tree about twenty feet from her.

She watched as two men walked up to him and roughly yanked him to his feet, then untied him. Another two came for her. She slid off the platform before they could have manhandled her. She hadn't bled any more since that first incident, and she wanted to keep it that way.

"Where are you taking us?" Jase demanded.

"To your lord and master," one of the men sneered.

"She shouldn't walk." Jase's voice was cold, thunder flashing across his face, the muscles in his arms flexing.

But the man just shrugged at him. "She looks fine to me. Move it."

Jase stepped toward her. The two men holding him pulled him back.

"Let me carry her." He switched to a more reasonable tone, trying another tactic. "Don't you have a wife at home?"

He received another shrug in response, but then he was released.

He immediately reached for her.

"You don't have to." She tried to step away from him.

She weighed a million pounds, and he'd been roughed up by a couple of thugs when they'd first arrived here. He'd demanded to be kept right next to her and had fought for it. Hadn't backed down until they'd tied him and beat him, then practically shoved a gun barrel up his nose.

"Jase, I can—"

She was in his arms before she could finish, and he stepped forward, carrying her as if she weighed nothing.

The weird thing was that, after about the first second, she didn't feel awkward. She put her arm around his neck and felt safe, grateful that he was here with her. If she and her baby survived this ordeal it would be thanks to God and Jase Campbell.

The men led him to the road that led to Pedro's camp. Some sort of signal was passed, and Cristobal's men surrounding the place stopped shooting. A few minutes passed before the enemy, too, fell silent.

"We have something that belongs to the Don," one of Cristobal's men shouted toward the closed gate, and shoved Jase out into plain sight. "Throw down your weapons and open the gate."

No response came.

The man nudged Jase forward. Melanie clung to his neck for dear life. The two of them against everyone else.

The silence stretched on.

Then the Don's men opened fire, obviously rejecting Cristobal's offer.

Jase dove into the bushes with her and kept going until they were safe. Their escort ran right behind them.

"Why didn't he want me back?" Her heartbeat galloped wildly. Pedro had told her a hundred times how important her child was to him. This didn't make any sense.

"Not what I expected either. But…" He shrugged. "Maybe he knows Cristobal's men would push through if he opened that gate. He knows Cristobal would execute him the second he had him. You and the baby are lost to him either way. His only chance for survival is to defend the compound to the last man." Jase carried her back to the camp and her platform, and laid her down.

A drizzle began to fall.

She rolled to her side to ease the pain in her lower back.

"Do you think Pedro knows the army is coming?" she asked.

"He might. But he might have something up his sleeve, too. He has many allies. Reinforcements could be on their way to him, just hours or minutes away."

She took a second to process that, then another few seconds passed before she could voice the question looming in her mind. "Will Cristobal kill us now?"

"I don't know," he called back as the men led him away.

He grabbed a faded green tarp from the ground as he walked, and they didn't take it away from him. He let them tie him up again, then lay down and covered himself against the slight drizzle. Only his legs and boots protruded. He shifted around a couple of times, probably trying to find a comfortable spot, but then stopped moving after a minute.

She couldn't comprehend how anyone could sleep in this melee with the threat of death hanging over his head.

She did her best to breathe deeply and evenly, trying to relax. She rubbed her belly. Beyond Cristobal, stress was the biggest threat to her and her baby at the moment. She couldn't do anything about Cristobal, but she could keep herself calm. She was still alive. Jase was still alive. A miracle could still happen.

She glanced over at him from time to time, finding his presence comforting. He'd walked next to her stretcher, as much as the narrow trail had allowed, all the way here. He'd kept her spirits up. He made sure the men took good care of her.

She was pretty sure he could have escaped a number of times, but he hadn't. She couldn't really understand why. She was nobody to him. He owed her nothing. His rescue complex couldn't be this strong—not stronger than the instinct for self-preservation.

She didn't want him to die because of her. He was a good man, better than any she'd known. His mission was important to the U.S. She hated the thought that she had messed that up for him. She wished there was something, anything, she could do to help, instead of being an ungainly ballast around his neck.

The drizzle picked up and turned into rain, the drops beating a monotone rhythm on the banana leaves above her, but it couldn't drown out the sounds of gunfire from the nearby siege. The rain didn't seem to bother the warring men.

She turned her head back to Jase. He hadn't moved since he'd fallen asleep. Something about that prickled her instincts. She'd never seen him that still. He was always alert; he practically slept with one eye open.

Was he hurt? For all she knew, the beating he'd received could have broken his ribs. That he'd carried her didn't mean he was okay. He had a tendency to ignore his injuries.

"Jase?" she called to him, but her voice was drowned out by a volley of gunfire and the rain.

She watched him, trying to determine if he was even breathing, but she was too far away to discern any movement. His pant legs were getting soaked. He'd lain down in an indentation in the ground between two palm trees, and now a puddle was forming under him. It amazed her that his wet clothes didn't wake him, or the water that had to be seeping into his boots.

His boots—

She stared through the rain, wanting to be sure. And after a few seconds, she was. Those weren't Jase's boots. His were black, and these were a worn brown. And all of a sudden she realized that the man's shape was off, too. Where were Jase's wide shoulders?

A second passed before she put together what must have happened. Jase had somehow grabbed a man at one point when nobody was looking, neutralized him and stashed the body under his tarp to give the appearance that he was still here. Then he'd taken off.

When? Why didn't he take her with him?

She looked around but couldn't see him lurking in the bushes. He was gone. The thought hit her hard in the middle of her chest.

First Mochi, then him. So self-preservation did trump everything, after all.

She couldn't blame them. She hoped, from the bottom of her heart, that both were safe somewhere far away from here. She would have run, too, if she was in any condition to do it.

As it was, she cradled her belly and listened to the battle, more scared than she'd ever been.

JASE STOLE FORWARD, probably faster than was strictly safe. He had to hurry. The army could be here any second, and once the reinforcements arrived, the attackers would storm the compound. Capturing the place shouldn't take too long with an overwhelming force like that.

Right now, Cristobal had a hundred other things beyond Melanie to think about. But once he'd taken the compound, he would remember her and get rid of the nuisance he had no use for whatsoever.

Jase sneaked around Don Pedro's camp in a wide circle. Cristobal's men surrounded it from every side. He looked for a weak point where he could break through, but he couldn't find any.

Fine. He'd make his own way.

He didn't dare leave Melanie alone for long.

He selected a man who squatted a little farther back in the bushes than the others, and sneaked up to him from behind as the guy shot a volley of bullets into the compound.

Jase slapped his left hand over the man's mouth from behind, yanked the guy's head back and cut his throat. He dumped the body into the bushes and took the guy's gun. He hadn't been able to get his own weapon back. Cristobal had taken a liking to it and had been walking around with the rifle on his shoulder the last time Jase had seen him.

The smaller weapon in his hand right now would have to do.

But he couldn't use it yet. He needed stealth a little longer.

He moved on to the next man. Broke his neck. Then he took out the next guy, then the next, a dozen of them altogether. The carnage didn't bother him. He was focused on the mission he was trying to accomplish.

Search and destroy. This was what he did. He was good at it.

He moved in a crouch toward the spot where he'd cut the hole in the fence before. The jungle reached all the way to the edge of the camp there, the easiest spot to break through, if he could get that far undetected.

God and luck and all the jungle spirits must have been with him because, against all odds, he did.

He crawled forward in the cover of the undergrowth as far as he dared, spotted Roberto peeking from behind the cover of the old shed on the other side of the fence and took him out with a single shot between the eyes. Then he neutralized two more of the Don's men.

He waited.

Nobody else seemed to be within sight of the path he planned to take. He pushed forward and through the hole in the fence, then ran to the cover of the old shed, stepping over the bodies of the men he'd killed.

The hacienda loomed two hundred yards from him.

Judging by the gunfire, there were about fifty people left inside the compound. They would all shoot him on sight if they spotted him. Alejandro would have gotten back to camp days ago and told them all that Jase was a traitor.

Cristobal had about a hundred men surrounding the place. Then there was the advancing army with at least two hundred soldiers.

When you were faced with overwhelming odds, the best thing to do was to focus on the basics. What were the things that were nonnegotiable, the priorities he *had* to achieve?

He had to take the compound and get Melanie inside somehow. She wasn't going to make it to the mission. She needed to be evacuated ASAP. For that, he needed one of Don Pedro's satellite phones so he could call in an evacuation team.

Beyond that, he needed to complete his mission. He needed names and dates on the planned insertion of terrorists onto U.S. soil. He needed Don Pedro's Mexican connection, the man on the border who would be smuggling the weapons and the terrorists through.

The easiest way to get the intel he needed would be to interrogate someone who had that information. But he couldn't just grab any guy. Not all of the Don's men would know about that business. In fact, most of them wouldn't. And he didn't have time to figure out who did. So he had to go for the obvious solution. The Don had the information, for sure.

Which meant that while he overtook the compound, he had to keep an eye out for the Don and grab him, and secure the man for extraction and interrogation when the evac team got here.

He rubbed his hand over his face and shook his head. Not that he didn't like a challenge…

He needed to buy some time. He rolled the half-formed ideas around in his head until they made sense.

He moved through the camp, always staying in cover, until he reached the back of the barracks. He slipped inside the empty building. Everybody had gone off to fight, it seemed, even the injured. He grabbed a piece of paper, a pen and some twine, then sat down to write, keeping the rifle in his left hand aimed at the door, should someone come in.

Señor Cristobal, we don't want this fight. Give us one hour of ceasefire to handle the men who are faithful to Don Pedro, then we will hand the camp and him over to you. There are twenty-three of us who would pledge our service to you.

He wrote in Spanish, making sure to misspell a couple of words as an uneducated bandit might, then signed Roberto's name.

Roberto had been close enough to the Don to conduct business on the man's behalf from time to time. He'd definitely be known to the Don's captains, and Cristobal had been one of those before he'd decided to take over the whole operation.

Jase slipped from the barracks the same way he'd sneaked in: unseen. He tied the note to a rock, then moved closer to the fence, waited for gunfire. He didn't have to wait long. He identified the shooter's location and threw the rock hard enough and far enough to hit the man. Of all the sports he'd played in high school and college, baseball had been his favorite. He'd been a pretty decent pitcher.

He heard a grunt as the stone hit its target, then he ducked to keep out of the way of the responding hail of bullets.

Then he waited, assessing the compound, noting the location of gunfire, guessing how many men manned the various posts around the perimeter. And he planned.

The battle went on for another twenty minutes before the attacking force fell silent little by little. Which meant his message had reached Cristobal at last.

He looked at his watch. He had one hour to take over the compound before Cristobal would attack again. Fighting one enemy at a time would be a lot easier.

He sneaked through the camp like a ghost, spotted several men, but avoided detection. Some seemed uneasy at the sudden end to the fighting and called for a small attack team to be sent out to see what was going on. Others were celebrating, assuming that Cristobal was ready to slink away defeated.

Jase headed to the packaging building. As sturdy as the hacienda itself, it had no windows and was guarded at all times. Except now. They needed every man for the fight.

He opened the padlock on the front door easily. He had made sure to find out the combination weeks ago, had searched the building once he'd managed to get the guard drunk in the middle of the night, in fact, but found nothing there beyond the drug stuff, nothing terrorist related.

Now he rushed in, having no time to waste, kicked over the nearest table and set it on fire. Then he went back to the entrance, made sure nobody saw him as he closed the door and used the doorknob to step up to the roof. He flattened himself and waited.

He didn't have to wait long. Soon smoke wafted through the rafters. He covered his mouth with his shirt. Another minute or two passed before someone noticed the smoke, then men were running to investigate, about a half dozen.

They noted the open padlock and pushed inside, saw the fire, rushed to beat it out. Jase couldn't see any others coming, so he jumped from the roof, slammed the door shut and clicked the padlock closed, trapping the bastards inside. Then he took off running, keeping in cover as much as possible.

The stables would have to be next, he decided, noting the three men who were taking a break in the shade by the front door. They didn't see him, or the fire, from where they were sitting. He sneaked inside from behind and pulled into the darkest corner, which smelled like hay and dung.

The mules didn't pay much attention to him. He'd taken care of them enough times for them to recognize him. They did smell the smoke, though, and were beginning to move around restlessly.

He checked his weapon, made sure he had enough bullets left in the magazine in case he needed the gun as a backup. On the first run, though, he preferred to try to take care of the men a little more quietly.

"What the hell is this?" he called out, making the question sound belligerent.

One of the men turned around, but couldn't see him in the deep shadows. "What?"

"Come and see."

The guy hesitated, but pushed to his feet. Jase waited until he was close enough, then grabbed him and silenced him with a quick stab of his knife between the man's ribs. Then he stole quietly forward to the other two, who were smoking and swearing about how damned tired they were, speculating about why they were suddenly getting a break.

He reached out and knocked their heads together, which stunned them for a second. He snapped the neck of one, then the other, and quickly pulled the bodies inside the building before anyone could have noticed.

He silently ticked off the head count. He'd made progress, but still had a long way to go.

He didn't enjoy killing. He did it as a last resort, when all his other options were exhausted. Taking a life wasn't something he did lightly. But when he had to do it, he could do it. He was a soldier. He'd been trained for this.

He needed to keep Melanie alive and capture the Don. Those were the only two things he was focused on now. He fixed them in his mind. Everything else was just details, steps to get through to achieve his objective.

He glanced at his watch. Fifteen minutes had passed since the guns had gone silent. Which meant he had forty-five minutes before the siege would start up again, everyone a lot more alert and shooting every which way.

He kept in cover as he stole toward the barracks. This time plenty of men were inside, taking advantage of the lull in the battle to eat and rest. He looked in through one of the windows, but couldn't see Consuela or any of the other women serving food. The women had probably left for the safety of the Jesuit mission when the shooting had started.

Cristobal would let them go. He might even hire them back when he took over the place. He had no quarrel with them.

Jase counted the men—almost a dozen, too many to just walk in and start an open confrontation. They all had their rifles by their sides. Chances were, a bullet would hit him before he could take all of them out. He couldn't lock them inside, either. The barracks had front and back doors, and windows. Not a place that could be easily secured.

After a few seconds of coming up with and discarding various plans, he moved back, deciding to save this problem for later.

He moved on to the dog enclosures, hoping he could make quick progress there. But he couldn't see anyone around. Some of the dogs barked a greeting; others had their tails tucked under them. They were used to guns going off, but not sustained gunfire, not battle like this. He patted a few that came over for reassurance, then kept going.

His best bet was to find men who were on their own or in groups of twos or threes and take them out a couple at a time. He moved toward the fence. There'd be men there, spread out, guarding the perimeter.

He began working on them, eliminating one after the other, almost on autopilot, working like a machine, moving forward, dealing with each threat as he came to it. He couldn't think of the number of lives he took. Not now. He would think about it, and deal with it, later.

When he finished with those who guarded the fence, he searched through camp and found and took out two more men. There were still that dozen in the barracks, and nearly as many up at the hacienda with the Don.

And as he went through his options once again, an idea occurred to him, a solution that would take care of half of his problems.

He sneaked over to the fuel storage shed where kerosene sat in metal barrels for the Don's generators, and filled up four cans. He carried the cans out. Tricky, since with two cans in each hand he had to carry his rifle on his shoulder, out of easy reach if he was spotted and attacked.

But his luck held.

He placed the full cans at the outside corners of the barracks, took off his shirt and ripped it into strips of various lengths. He tucked one end of a strip into each can, then lit the fabric with his lighter, creating supersized Molotov cocktails with some extra-long fuses. He needed that to time the explosions.

And he did calculate right. This wasn't his first rodeo. The makeshift bombs went off one right after the other, just seconds after he pulled back and took cover.

The explosion opened up the building, the roof disappearing, the walls shredded. The few men who lived were injured badly enough so they would be no threat to Jase, or anyone else, in the near future.

He glanced at his watch. Thirty minutes had passed. He had thirty more to finish what he'd started.

He watched from his hiding place as men rushed from the hacienda, drawn by the explosion. They didn't approach the burning barracks to save their injured comrades. Instead, they looked around in panic, guns aimed every which way as they tried to spot Cristobal's invading forces. Then they spotted the burning packaging building in the back and stared at it, bewildered.

"Where are the bastards?" one shouted.

When they didn't see an immediate threat, they pulled back into the hacienda. They didn't dare to cut across the compound to help their compadres. They knew the enemy was close, but they couldn't see it, which seemed to thoroughly unsettle them.

The front door closed behind the cowardly group. Gun barrels appeared in the windows next.

The Don was making his last stand in there with the dozen or so men he had left. They would defend the place down to the last man. Unfortunately, Jase needed a satellite phone and he needed the Don, and both were in there.

He couldn't attempt a frontal assault. He'd be dead the second he stepped out of cover.

The roof would have been a good entry point, but first he would have had to get up there. No tall trees stood around the hacienda. And he couldn't climb the walls, because he couldn't reach the walls, not from any side. He would have been immediately picked off by one of those rifles in the windows.

Okay, so he wasn't going to be able to take the hacienda by force, not without help. What did that leave him?

If he was going to get in, he had to talk those men into letting him in. It pretty much came down to that.

He took a minute to think that through, then he pulled back to the burning ruins of the barracks, stayed out of sight of the men at the hacienda as he focused on the wreckage.

He could see three injured men who'd crawled away from the explosion in one piece. He picked the closest one, smeared the man's blood all over his own face until he figured his features would be unrecognizable. Then he picked up the semiconscious man and stepped out from cover to run toward the hacienda, screaming in Spanish.

"Let me in! He's still alive. Help!"

He held the man in a way that if the others opened fire on him, the guy would block most of the bullets, at least to Jase's crucial organs. He also made sure to run close enough to cover so that he could lunge to safety the second any bullets began to fly.

But nobody fired on him. He reached the door safely, and then someone from the inside yanked it open for him.

He registered the two men he faced. Both had their weapons drawn, but their rifles were aimed behind Jase, at a possible enemy that might choose this vulnerable moment to attack.

Jase threw the man he carried on one of the Don's foot soldiers, then pulled up his gun and shot the other. The man he'd knocked over recovered quickly and went for his own weapon. Jase squeezed off a shot first. He hit his target, but he didn't have time to stop and celebrate.

Others ran forward and opened fire. He ducked through a doorway and behind a wall that kept him safe. He listened for every shot, memorized the location of every single shooter as best he could.

Then he popped out and took out the closest shooter before pulling back into safety. He let a full minute pass, let them waste a few dozen bullets. Then he took out the next man, then the next.

The rest were starting to get nervous, judging by all the swearing and shouting. They hadn't recognized him, not yet, not with his face obscured.

When new shots came, they came from farther away. The men were retreating up the stairs.

He scanned the room he was in: furniture turned over, empty ammo boxes scattered. No sight of a satellite phone in here. He glanced out into the main room, couldn't see a phone there, either. He had taken the lower level of the house, but everything he wanted was upstairs.

And he couldn't take the stairs. He'd have to come out into the open first, and the men at the top of the stairs would have higher ground. Plus he was outnumbered. His enemies had every advantage.

Still, he'd gotten this far. He refused to fail now.

He simply needed a new plan. He thought of Melanie out there with Cristobal and came up with one in a hurry.

Instead of pushing forward, he pulled farther back, all the way to the window at the back of the room. He opened it and looked up to the window above him. No gun barrel protruded from there. Chances were, the Don had every available man guarding the stairs, expecting the intruder to attack there.

Jase climbed out, then up, climbed through the upstairs window, and silently stole across the room he found himself in. Then he was at his enemies' back and opened fire, killing the men at the top of the stairs with one long, continuous burst of bullets.

As a maneuver it was damn fine and effective, but his luck finally ran out just then. A bullet had slammed into his side. Another grazed his shoulder.

He ignored both injuries as he scanned his surroundings. The door to the Don's office was closed. He would be in there—he wasn't among the dead at the top of the stairs. But how many men did he have with him?

However many, they would be securing the door. The Don would be cowering somewhere in the back, Jase reasoned, and he sprayed the door with bullets. Then, without leaving anyone in there a chance to recover, he rushed forward, kicked the door in and burst through it.

Pain shot through his side, through the bullet wound, nearly blinding him for a minute. He shook his head and got his vision back.

Dead men littered the floor. Alejandro stood in the far corner protecting the Don, who was trying to get through the window. Alejandro aimed and squeezed the trigger, but nothing happened. He shook his jammed weapon as he swore, his face red, his eyes bugging out with rage as he recognized Jase.

Shooting at Alejandro was out of the question. Too much of a chance that the bullet would go straight through him and hit the Don, too. Jase couldn't afford to sacrifice that asset.

He lunged at the two men and brought them down. Snapped his head up and caught the Don in the chin, smashing the man's head against the floor and knocking him out temporarily.

Alejandro didn't allow himself to be subdued that easily. Since his weapon had been knocked from his hand, he went for his knife and sliced into the side of Jase's neck, nearly taking off his ear.

Jase fought back with everything he had. Damn, but rolling on the floor hurt like hell. He was pretty sure he had a couple of cracked ribs from the beating he'd received from Cristobal's men. The bullet hole in his side stabbed with pain. But if he didn't win here, things would get a lot worse than that.

Alejandro outweighed him by at least thirty pounds and carried the fury of several grudges against him, which gave the guy extra strength. Plus he'd been resting for the past hour while Jase had been taking out one man after the other.

Alejandro pinned him to the floor and had his knife

at Jase's throat the next second. "Traitor," he hissed, and went for the kill.

But Jase rolled him and grabbed for the knife, twisted the man's wrist, and pushed the blade through Alejandro's black heart.

Then pulled it out and pushed it in again, just to be sure.

He didn't wait until the man bled out and stopped breathing. He went to tie up the Don just as the man was coming to. The boss swore like the bandit he was, spouting off one threat after the other. Jase wasn't in the mood to listen. He gagged the bastard, then grabbed the satellite phone from the bed and called the colonel at last, moving out of the room and down the stairs.

He gave his coordinates first to make sure they had that, even if the call somehow got disconnected.

"Also there's an army unit of roughly two hundred soldiers to the north of here, ready to join the fight. If they reach us, it's all over, sir." He ran for the hole in the fence as he talked.

"What's the army doing getting involved in a drug battle?"

"Cristobal might have bought off a general." Unfortunately, those sorts of things happened around here.

A moment of silence passed. "Don't worry about the army. I'll deal with that via official channels. What do you need?"

"An evac chopper with medical personnel on board. I have a pregnant woman here who's not doing well. I also have Don Pedro in custody."

"Well done. How long can you hold your position?"

He thought of Cristobal's men and the army that

might or might not arrive at any minute. "An hour or two at the most. And that's pretty damn optimistic."

"You hang in there. Help is on the way."

"One more thing, sir. Do you think the chopper could bring about a dozen dog cages?"

He ended the call before any questions could be asked about that, and ran through the camp, scanning his surroundings to make sure he hadn't missed anyone. He dashed straight to the hole in the fence, then through it.

Cristobal's men would be attacking again soon, when they realized that the Don's men weren't defecting and handing the boss over to him after all.

Jase glanced at his watch.

He had ten more minutes.

Chapter Eleven

Jase made his way to Cristobal's makeshift headquarters, staying out of sight. He checked the tree he'd been tied to. The body was still where he'd left it, covered with the tarp. Good. That meant that his absence hadn't been discovered.

At least not by Cristobal's men.

Melanie kept scanning the forest. Sure looked like she'd somehow noticed the switch and was wondering where he'd gone. When she looked his way, he quickly showed himself and gestured to her to come to him before pulling back behind the wall of green.

She immediately sat up and slid to the ground.

One of the soldiers confronted her. "You stay right there."

She lifted her hand to her mouth and swayed on her feet. "I'm going to throw up. The baby is pushing on my stomach. I'm just going over to those bushes." She heaved toward him.

The man stepped back and gave her an annoyed look, but didn't stop her when she moved forward.

Jase kept his gun ready in case anyone came after her. Nobody did. She walked slowly, with an exaggerated waddle, as if to make sure that nobody who looked at her would even think of the possibility that she might run away.

Then she reached him, and he stepped back so she could move deeper into cover before he picked her up and carried her off unseen.

"You came back." She sounded relieved, but maybe a twinge surprised, too. "Why? I'm nobody to you."

"You're not nobody," he groused, annoyed that she would think he might leave her. "Either we both make it out of here, or die trying."

"I vote for option number one."

He looked into her eyes and wanted to kiss her more than he had ever wanted to do anything. "Smart woman." He pushed forward. They were out of time.

Cristobal's men were heading back to the gate, but he still had a clear path to the hole in the fence. Jase remained alert, ready to set her down and go for his gun at a moment's notice.

"Where is everyone? Why are we going in there?" she asked when they reached the camp's perimeter.

"It's all ours now. The evac chopper is on the way."

Her eyes went wide. "How?"

"Don't worry about it. Your only job is to stay calm and well for the baby."

Then they were through the hole, and he covered it with some branches. He picked her up again on the other side. He kept in the cover of the buildings, just in case, and reached the hacienda safely. He set her down in the nearest chair inside and barred the front door behind them.

"I can't believe we're back here." She looked around, chagrin on her face. "After all I've done to get away from this place."

"You sit and relax. I'll take you up to your room in a minute."

He ran up and dragged two dead bodies out of her room. The blood on the floor couldn't be helped. But he had a feeling she would deal with it, like she had dealt with everything else. Gunfire sounded in the distance. Cristobal was getting impatient.

He rushed down for her and carried her up, set her on the bed. Then he pushed her rustic, solid wood armoire in front of the window so there wouldn't be any flying glass from bullets. "You relax. Help will be here before you know it."

He checked in on the Don tied up in his bedroom. The man shot him murderous looks but couldn't do much else. Then Jase ran back downstairs and secured all the doors and windows, and blocked all the downstairs entrances into the house with whatever furniture was at hand.

He collected all the guns and ammunition from the bodies in the process, then stockpiled them around the windows upstairs. He ended up with considerable firepower. The bag of hand grenades he found in one of the rooms was gravy.

His hour had been up ten minutes ago. Cristobal's men were probably at the gate, waiting for the handover.

Jase watched from the window he picked for his first station, ready for them if they started rolling down the path that led to the hacienda. Had he more time, he could have rigged some explosives and booby traps. But no one ever had enough time to do everything on an op. You did the best you could and made sure it was enough.

Rifle fire sounded from the direction of the gate. Then more guns from the back. The battle was back on.

The men would soon figure out that nobody was returning fire. But they would still move slowly, careful in case they faced some kind of a trap.

Long minutes passed before Jase saw the first of them, keeping low, keeping in cover. Then others came, clearing one building after the other, kicking the bodies on the ground to make sure they were really dead. When they were close enough to the hacienda so that Jase knew every one of his bullets would find its target, he opened fire.

He stood in one of the front corner rooms that had one window looking to the front, the other one to the side, so he could single-handedly keep two sides of the building protected. He laid down some serious fire, then ran to the Don's office, the corner room in the back, and did the same there.

Cristobal's men pulled back. They had no idea how many enemies were holed up in the house, but they could see it was a well-defensible position. Jase had the higher ground and solid cover, while they would have to come out in the open to reach the place.

He alternated among the dozen windows, exchanging fire with the enemy as they continued searching the camp. Half an hour passed as more and more men arrived and took up positions around the hacienda. If they decided to rush the place all at once, he was finished. The key was to make them think the Don had overwhelming force inside the building, dozens of men who could hold their positions indefinitely.

The fighters outside tested him, varying the direction and the intensity of the attacks. He stood up to the test, guessing their every move before they made it.

"Hand over the Don," came the demand from behind a stack of logs, at last.

Jase answered it with a hail of bullets. He needed a good show of strength. His ribs hurt, blood seeped from the bullet hole in his side. He drank to replenish fluids, but couldn't do much beyond that.

Time seemed to crawl. Exhaustion slowed him, and the evac team was still at least an hour away.

So when Cristobal himself called out, "All I want is the Don," Jase responded.

"Okay, okay. Give us some time to talk about this."

He used this new ceasefire to drink some more water and check on Melanie.

She looked pale and uncomfortable.

"Are you in pain?"

She looked away from him. "No."

His muscles tensed. "Where does it hurt?"

"I'll be fine."

"I need to know what's going on with you. It's the only way I can plan for all contingencies."

She looked at her feet. "I think that spotting in the forest might have been the mucus plug."

He cringed. Maybe he shouldn't have pushed for the answer. Sounded like one of those feminine mystery things a man was better off not knowing about. But because it concerned *her,* he asked anyway. "The what?"

"It usually indicates the beginning of labor."

He stopped breathing there for a second. "Have you had any contractions?"

She didn't say anything.

"Melanie?"

"Yes."

Cold fear cut through him. He would rather have

faced a force twice as large as Cristobal's, with tanks, than have to be within ten miles of a woman in labor. "Are you sure?"

She had the presence and energy to laugh at him.

Good to know that one of them still had their sense of humor.

A million questions flew threw his head. Somehow he managed to articulate one. "How soon will the baby come?"

"I don't think these things can be predicted."

"Can you hold it in?"

"Yeah." She laughed again. "How about I cross my legs?"

He glared at her for making fun of him. "Call me if you need me," he said, then fled to check on the Don, his mind a beehive of unsettling thoughts and images.

The drug boss growled at him from behind the gag as Jase stepped into the room. Blind, dark fury clouded his eyes. He would have killed Jase if he could. And yet, at the moment, Jase felt more comfortable in this room than in the other one. Violence he understood. He had skills to deal with that. He had no idea what to do with a laboring woman.

"Relax, amigo." He passed by the man. "Right now, I'm the only thing standing between you and Cristobal, who wants to tear you limb from limb."

He checked outside from each window, scanned the camp in every direction. Cristobal's men kept in cover, but were relaxed. Some were even smoking. They didn't think they needed to keep their locations concealed. While the exchange of gunfire had shown them that the hacienda was well-defended, from the number of bodies around the camp they had pretty much figured

out that the Don wouldn't have a large enough force
left to risk a breakout and try to match the invading
force man for man.

Jase checked his guns, made sure they were all
loaded, then checked in on Melanie again. Again, she
insisted that she was fine, not that he bought it. The
tight lines of tension around her eyes told another story.

The grace period of this latest ceasefire lasted about
half an hour before Cristobal lost his patience and ordered another attack.

It started out badly. A bullet grazed Jase's left eyebrow almost immediately. Other than ripping off half
the eyebrow, it wasn't a big deal, but then blood began
trickling into his eye. And the men were shooting like
crazy. He didn't have time to stop and stanch the wound
with a makeshift bandage. He kept wiping it with the
back of his hand and blinking, but the dripping blood
interfered with his vision and his aim. Which slowed
his return fire.

The bastards outside thought that the inside force
was weakening and launched an all-around attack—
just what he didn't need.

Pretty soon, the enemy figured out that there weren't
as many people inside the hacienda as they had thought,
and pushed forward all at once, from every direction.
The fight reached a critical point. The battle could be
lost in minutes if he couldn't hold the attackers back.

Then Melanie appeared in the doorway. "I want to
help."

"Go back to bed. You need to stay off your feet." He
kept shooting.

"If they break into the house, none of that is going
to matter."

He gritted his teeth. "Can you handle a gun?"

"You could teach me."

"No time for that."

"I have a good arm."

"What?"

"Baseball. I played on the women's team at the university."

He glanced back. Maybe she was delirious from pain.

But she shuffled closer, grabbed a grenade from the floor next to him—he'd been saving those for later—pulled the pin, popped up from behind him and let the grenade fly.

She'd aimed at a group of men who'd been shooting the house from behind a pile of wood. The grenade cleared the stack of logs and went down right behind it. The force of the explosion sent three men into the air.

"It doesn't hurt all the time," she said behind him. "Just the contractions. I feel fine in-between." She lobbed another grenade.

He stared at her, frankly filled with admiration. "Look at you now."

She put her chin up. "I'm done hiding behind other people's backs."

He squeezed off a couple of rounds before he responded. "Go to the back of the house. Take as many grenades as you can. And sit down, for heaven's sake." He couldn't really afford to take his eyes off the enemy, but he glanced back anyway and caught her gaze one more time. "Be careful."

"I'm fighting for my baby," she said, as she gathered up two dozen grenades in her shirt.

Which gave him an idea. He squeezed off a few more rounds, then ran off to grab the Don and drag him back to the front room with him. He pulled the rag from the man's mouth.

"This is how it's going to go. I shoot, you throw the grenades."

"Who the hell are you?" The man's eyes blazed with heat.

They had no time for that. "These are your choices: if Cristobal gets his hands on you, you're dead. You help me fight him off, and you'll get a comfortable cell in a U.S. prison, three square meals, cable TV, you can go to college and get a law degree or whatever."

The Don looked like he was ready to strangle him. But he nodded. He probably figured he'd get away from Jase later. "Give me a gun."

"I don't think so." A gun could be too easily turned against him. But if the Don dropped a grenade in the room, they'd both be killed. He untied the man's hands, ready for an attack, but the Don seemed smart enough to have gotten his point. Good. "Aim and throw. Get busy."

The attackers were getting too damned close to the building.

Melanie was holding off the men in the back, though. Explosions shook the air regularly, coming from that direction.

The three of them working together pushed back the next wave of attack successfully.

But as much as having the Don helped, he also slowed Jase down, since he had to keep an eye on the man and he could no longer run from room to room to check all around the building without dragging the guy behind him.

And that was a giant drawback, he acknowledged silently, as a loud crash came from below.

Jase swore. That had to be one of the boarded-up windows. Somebody had just made his way in.

Their defenses had been breached.

And the evac team was still nowhere in sight.

Chapter Twelve

Defending the top of the stairs was the name of the game at this stage, so Jase rushed to take that strategic position, taking the Don with him. The man had stuffed his pockets full of grenades, so he was supplied for a while.

Melanie limped down the hall for more hand grenades, then went to cover the area outside the breached window so no additional attackers could come in. Jase couldn't believe she could still think at this stage, let alone put up a fight.

He couldn't watch her for long. He had to turn his attention back to the melee. Then a shout from the Don distracted him for a second from the man who'd broken through and had now taken up position downstairs.

One of his bullets hit the Don in the shoulder and he went down. Right shoulder. He wouldn't be much help after this. Which was fine. Too many hand grenades going off inside the house wouldn't be a good thing anyway. The explosions could weaken the structure enough so the whole building would collapse.

At least the army had never materialized, Jase thought, trying to think of some silver lining. Maybe they were on the take from both sides. He needed something good to hang on to.

Then he finally got a clean shot of the man below and took him out. The enemy fighter went down, leaving red splash marks behind him on the wall.

Not wanting to waste the momentary break, Jase ran to Melanie.

"Still okay?"

"First babies don't come so fast. Quit worrying."

He ran to the other side of the house to look out that way. Men were right up by the wall, trying to breach another boarded-up window. There were probably more up front, doing the same. He pointed his gun out and down and shot randomly, scattering them. When they returned fire, he pulled back in and ran to the front to do some damage control there, but was stopped halfway by a keening sound.

Melanie.

He changed course immediately. "Are you hit?"

No answer came.

THE SUDDEN CONTRACTION took her breath away. This was different than the others. This one meant it.

She dropped the grenade, just barely outside the window. It blew up right at the foot of the wall and shook the building. Okay, she was now officially doing more damage than good. Time to quit.

Even from her sitting position she could see Cristobal's men rush in from every direction. They knew the defense team was weakening, and they were moving in for the kill.

There were too many of them. She could hear them

breaking through the boarded-up windows and coming in downstairs.

"I'm coming," Jase shouted to her, but from the sound of his gun, she figured he'd been stopped at the top of the stairs, trying to hold them back from coming up.

She could no longer help. She glanced at the Don's bed in the far corner and stood from the chair to waddle over there. Her water broke halfway to her destination.

She braced her back against the wall as another contraction gripped her. The baby was definitely coming.

She desperately wanted to live long enough to see her son born. When the contraction passed, she moved forward. A short burst of gunfire sounded just outside her door. Then silence.

Was Jase hit? She detoured that way with what little strength she had left.

"Get back!" he yelled as soon as he spotted her. "I got this."

His tone and expression were grim. He was bleeding from several wounds, his face was messed up.

Her heart turned over in her chest. He was protecting her to his dying breath, like he'd promised. She'd never met anyone like him. In another life...if things had been different...

But no amount of valor could stand against the overwhelming force they faced. Tears burned her eyes as she realized they weren't going to make it.

She could see out the front window from where she stood. More of Cristobal's thugs were rushing toward the hacienda. Trying to get to the bed no longer mattered, so she simply leaned against the wall and looked at Jase. At best, they had minutes left to live.

But then she saw something strange happen outside. One of the attacking men in the back of the group fell and didn't get up. Definitely not Jase's doing. He had his gun trained on the stairs inside.

Then she saw another of Cristobal's men fall outside, then another, taken out by a phantom enemy from the forest. Yet she heard no gunfire coming from the jungle.

Maybe she was hallucinating out of sheer desperation, seeing what she wanted to see.

But soon half a dozen men were on the ground. Then a dozen. Their buddies up front realized at that point what was going on, turned to shoot at the forest, abandoning their attack of the hacienda. They looked bewildered, firing wildly, not particularly aiming at anything.

It seemed as if the forest itself had risen up against them and fought against them with some ancient magic.

She felt as stunned as they had to be, the short hairs rising at her nape. Then she saw a brownish shape fall from one of the trees. She couldn't make out who he was until he hit the ground: a native Indian, dressed in nothing but a loincloth. He still clutched the blowpipe he'd been using as a weapon. He stayed where he'd dropped, unmoving, red blooming on his chest.

Some tribal warriors had arrived, fighting with poison darts. Probably from one of the nearby villages. It made no sense. According to Pedro, they avoided him and his men, the loggers and the drug runners. She could understand why: Pedro and the men he employed gave nothing to those villagers but grief.

Yet they were here now, invisible in the trees, and they had very accurate aim. They were bringing down Cristobal's men one after the other. The bandits were still spraying the trees blindly with their automatic weapons. And the sheer volume of bullets was starting to show results. Several of the native warriors fell as she watched helplessly, contractions gripping her.

She slid to the floor, doing whatever Lamaze breathing she'd seen on TV. She hadn't gone to actual classes yet. Nor would she get to, at this stage. *Too late,* she thought. *Too late for everything.*

Then, after what seemed an eternity, Jase's gun fell silent at the top of the stairs. And soon the guns outside, too, quieted.

"I think whoever the Indians didn't get ran off." Jase picked her up and carried her to the closest room with a bed: Pedro's. She was beyond caring.

He left, but came back a minute later dragging the Don behind him. He tied the injured man up and shoved him into the corner without ceremony.

Then he turned to her, his gaze immediately softening. "Sorry. Can't afford to let him run off at this stage."

"Please. Not here." She had her limits.

He nodded after a moment and dragged the man out, came back in shortly. "Tied him up in his office and locked him in. How are you?"

Breathing hard. "How soon is that chopper coming?"

He looked her over, the way her face twisted with the next contraction, his gaze falling to the hand that held her belly. "Probably not soon enough." A twinge of panic underlined his words.

She wasn't used to seeing him unsettled, his unbreakable composure shaken. Made him a little more approachable, actually.

"I'll be fine. Women have been doing this since the beginning of time." Whatever confidence she didn't feel, she faked.

He laid his gun down, but didn't step closer.

She gulped some air. "At least that's what they always say on TV in situations like this."

He flashed a pained grin.

Then spun and went for his gun. But didn't shoot.

Mochi stood in the door. The kid was smiling from ear to ear, his chest puffed out a mile. He sauntered in, surveyed the situation, then moved to the window and shouted a couple of sentences in his native language.

Jase went to look out from behind him. A strange look crossed his face as he surveyed whatever was going on out there.

She wanted to see, too, but couldn't get up. Not even between two contractions now. They were too close together. "What's happening?"

"About two dozen warriors are picking up their dead. They are pulling back into the forest."

Mochi came to her, a proud smile on his face.

"Oh, Mochi." Tears sprung to her eyes. "You are really something. Thank you. You saved our lives, you know that?"

Then she couldn't say anything for a while as the next contraction came.

"I think we're going to need clean water and clean sheets," she said when the contraction passed.

"More TV wisdom?"

She flinched.

"I don't suppose you took one of those classes?"

"I was going to do that after I got back from delivering Julio's ashes to his family." That trip didn't turn out as planned, to say the least.

He raked his long fingers through his hair. "You should puff your cheeks out. I mean breathe."

"You think?"

He'd gone from supersoldier to rattled man pretty quickly, clearly out of his element with the whole childbirth thing.

"I'm going to help," he said heroically, even as his eyes said he wanted to run for the hills.

"I appreciate it."

But someone else showed up before he would have been put to the test. An old Indian woman appeared in the doorway.

Mochi greeted her respectfully. She measured up the situation, looked out the window as if orienting herself, then picked a corner and set down her bundle, pulling out a dried birdwing with the black feathers still attached to it.

She swept out the corner with it, then reached to her waist and unwrapped her skirt, laying the reddish colored cloth down. Now she stood there in nothing but a loincloth that was way too skimpy in the back—just a stringy thing, really, revealing way too much sagging and wrinkly skin.

Not that Melanie would have criticized her for anything. She was so grateful for help she could have wept.

Jase, who'd stared at first, then turned away, not knowing where to look, snapped back to the task at hand at last. "Where are the towels?"

"I have fresh sheets in my armoire."

He shot out of the room.

Mochi just kept grinning, a pleased look on his face. All was well in his book. They'd been saved and he'd somehow even gotten a medicine woman here. He didn't seem uncomfortable with the whole giving-birth thing.

Melanie had the sudden thought that being a child of a close-knit village, the boy might have seen dozens of babies born. Certainly more than she and Jase.

His optimism was beginning to rub off on her. He really was an exceptional little boy.

"Any mother would be proud to have a son like you, you know that?" she told him in between contractions.

The medicine woman seemed to be done with her preparation, because she came over to the bed and looked into Melanie's eyes. And for a moment the room and everyone else disappeared. Melanie felt pulled into a swirl of soothing murmurs, although the woman's lips didn't move.

Oh, God. Exhaustion was making her loopy, she thought, more than a little discombobulated.

Then the woman broke eye contact, and the strange dizzy sensation immediately disappeared. She said something to Mochi. The boy left the room.

Jase checked in with those sheets, still looking nervous around the edges.

The woman motioned him inside, then did the eye-lock with him next, cocking her head to the right, staring at his face unblinking as if wanting to see inside him. He looked almost hypnotized, as if compelled not to look away.

The strange spectacle lasted only a few seconds. Then the woman gestured to him, indicating that he should pick up Melanie and carry her to the cloth she'd laid out. She made him sit down, too, his back braced against the corner of the room. Then she manipulated Melanie until she was sitting between Jase's pulled-up knees, her back braced against his bare chest.

She would have much rather stayed in the bed, but she was beyond protesting. A contraction gripped her. She couldn't breathe for a minute.

"It's too early." The woman simply nodded, reached into a pouch that hung from a cord tied around her waist, and sprinkled some dried herbs around them while muttering the same few words toward the north, east, west and south.

Mochi came back with water, then went out again.

The woman put a different kind of herb into the bowl, mixed it up with her hands. The water turned red. Then she removed Melanie's pants and underwear without ceremony, pushed her legs up and began to wash her. Her skin turned red wherever the herbal water touched it.

Talk about embarrassing. She couldn't look at Jase. Hoped he had his eyes closed.

"What is she doing?" she asked him under her breath.

"Whatever it is, her people have probably been doing it for thousands of years. She's probably using some astringent plant juice to fight against bacteria."

Whether he was right or not, it sounded good. The room was far from sterile.

By the time the medicine woman finished, the contractions came one on the heel of the other. The baby seemed to be in a rush. Was that a good sign or a bad one?

"Where is the evacuation team?" she demanded, expectation mixing with fear.

Jase held her against his body, held her up. "On their way. Hang in there. We'll do this together."

If embarrassment didn't kill her first. She only hoped that where he sat behind her, he couldn't see her naked bottom half. She tried to move her head into position to block his line of vision and make sure.

But when the medicine woman finished with another batch of incantations, she grabbed the edge of Melanie's T-shirt and pulled it over her head before she had a chance to protest.

"No, no, no."

Too late.

Another contraction gripped her, and she was helpless as the woman divested her of her bra, which had been her very last stich of clothing. This was so wrong on so many levels. She couldn't protect herself. All she could do was wrap her arms around her chest.

"Relax," Jase said from behind her. "You're okay."

"I'm naked!"

"I noticed." His voice was a notch lower as he said that. "Think of it as natural."

"As long as you don't think of it at all."

A second passed. His fingers brushed against the spot between her shoulder blades. "You have a tattoo."

"Not going to talk about that right now."

He brushed over it again. "Okay. But we're definitely talking about it later."

The woman prepared a thicker concoction, also red, and dipped her fingers into it to draw circles around Melanie's stomach, then her breasts, all the while murmuring. Then she drew geometric signs over the circles, until her skin was covered and she looked like she was wearing paint-on clothes.

It kind of made her feel a little less naked. Or maybe she was beyond the point of caring.

The contractions were hard enough by now that she could no longer focus on anything other than the baby coming. She gripped Jase's hands, feeling as if she were about to burst.

The woman pulled out another roll of bunched-up dried herbs, took a beat-up cigarette lighter out of her pocket that seemed ridiculously out of place and lit the end of the bundle, then circled the smoke around Melanie.

She tried to hold her breath at first, but could only do it for so long. With the next contraction, she had to breathe. The smoke smelled sweet. Settled into her lungs. And eased the pain.

The woman's incantations got louder, not shouting but rather vibrating, into her, through her. The sound waves rocked her, soothed her. Soon she felt as if her body bobbed on top of ocean waves. She could feel her baby and his strong heartbeat, felt Jase's heart beat against her back, mixing with hers and the baby's, the three distinct rhythms harmonizing.

For a second she felt that she was melding with Jase's body, even as the baby melded with hers.

Then a sudden urge came to push, and she did, bracing her back against Jase, pushing back against him, holding on to his hands, digging her heels into the floor.

"There you go. You can do this," he murmured into her ear, his voice soft and encouraging.

The urge passed and she rested for a minute before the next came. And the next, and the next.

She grunted hard with the last one.

Then the baby was in her arms, naked and slippery against her skin.

She looked into her son's eyes. She reveled in the sight of his perfect nose and lips as the medicine woman tied off the umbilical cord and took care of everything.

Her son—small, but alert and breathing just fine, holding on to her pinky finger. She glanced back over her shoulder at Jase. He looked stunned, his eyes suspiciously glistening, filled with awe and wonder.

All his hard edges were gone, all his shadows. He looked as if he'd just witnessed a miracle.

She was pretty sure they all did.

HE FELT AS if he'd just given birth, a darn strange thing, not something he would have believed if anyone had said something like this to him. Melanie held her baby, and he held Melanie. The sense of oneness was palpable, an overwhelming, almost surreal feeling.

She was naked and in his arms, but there was nothing sexual about the moment. The emotions he felt were primal, elemental, overpowering.

Dozens of half-formed thoughts swirled in his mind, but only one was coherent: *they were his.*

The old woman cleaned the baby without removing him from Melanie's arm, took care of the afterbirth, said more prayers or whatever it was she was doing. He didn't move, unwilling to break the bond, but when the sound of a chopper filled the air, he did let them go at last, laying her down gently before he pushed to his feet.

"I better check outside."

Melanie just looked at him, as if not registering his words. He couldn't blame her.

He walked out to the balcony, his knees shaky for the first time that he could remember, then stepped up onto the railing and from there onto the roof, and searched the sky, a different man from the one who'd called for rescue.

Somehow the last hour had changed everything.

He spotted the chopper, waved, and the camouflaged bird began to lower toward the clearing in the middle of the camp. Men holding guns poured out, secured the area immediately before heading for the hacienda.

By the time he climbed down and went back to Melanie, she was wrapped in a clean sheet, her baby bundled in with her. She looked up at him, her eyes moist. "Isn't he perfect?"

"Perfect."

"Thank you. We wouldn't have made it without you," she told him.

But the tender moment they shared ended too quickly.

Soldiers rushed in with guns drawn. Jase identified himself and waved them right back out, letting only the medic in. The guy looked at the blood seeping from Jase's side and reached for his bag.

"Touch me and lose the hand," Jase warned him. "You can look at me when she's safe in a hospital bed. Your patient is over there."

The man held up his hands and backed toward Melanie.

Jase went outside with the others and told them what had happened, told them about the dogs and where the drugs and guns were hidden, then he dragged the Don out to them. Two men picked up the drug boss and carried him to the chopper unceremoniously while the Don threatened every one of them, alternating with offers of bribes, the size of which would have made the average man gasp. They all ignored him.

Jase stood on the hacienda's steps and looked out at the dozen men who were clearing the compound building by building, looking for enemy fighters who might still be alive despite their injuries.

The carnage had been incredible. Between himself and Mochi's people, they'd taken out a hundred drug runners. If he hadn't seen it, he wouldn't have thought it possible.

The Don was in custody. Cristobal, if he had somehow survived, might never recover from his losses. There were others like them out there, too many to count, but for now, for here, there would be peace. The days of gunfire had ended, the jungle around them was quiet.

He hadn't envisioned his mission ending like this, but he couldn't say he was disappointed.

He walked up to the packaging building, where men

were digging up the carefully packaged bricks of cocaine.

"We can use the hole to bury the dead," he told them. "There are indigenous tribes around here. We don't want to leave any decomposing bodies around to spread disease."

Then he moved on to inspect the bodies, looking for Cristobal. But he couldn't find the man anywhere inside the camp, and not out in the forest, either.

Still, they had closed down the compound and captured the Don. A huge step in the right direction. The blow dealt to the drug and gun trade would reverberate through the organization.

By the time he walked back to the hacienda, men were carrying Melanie and the baby to the chopper on a stretcher.

Mochi followed.

The kid had saved their lives, no doubt about it.

"Gracias." Jase put a hand on the boy's shoulder and pointed to the chopper with a questioning look. He had an aunt back in the States who lived on a farm—lots of green, lots of trees, animals. A kid could be happy there, he thought. He would stop by every chance he got. He would take care of Mochi. He would do whatever it took to make sure he was cared for and safe.

They could go hiking together when he was on leave. Now that he thought of it, he liked that picture, looked forward to introducing Mochi to another kind of forest. The boy could discover things along with his aunt's grandkids.

But Mochi simply touched his hand to the baby's shoulder, then Melanie's. Then he gave a solemn look to Jase and turned back toward the forest where the warriors waited for him. They might have been from another village, but they were likely the same tribe, an extended family.

A sharp sense of loss sliced through Jase, but he held still, didn't call Mochi back. Even he could see that this was better for the kid. He blinked once. Hard.

"Wait," he called after the boy, then pulled his best knife from his boot and presented it to the kid.

Not something he would have done back home, but this was a different world. Here, Mochi was a warrior now at age six, doubly so because he'd saved lives and taken them, too. He had to have fought in the battle, otherwise he wouldn't be here now. The warriors didn't bring along spectators.

He accepted the knife with the biggest smile on his face and seemed to grow an inch. A warrior's weapons added greatly to his status. And now he had the best knife in a hundred-mile radius, probably. A valued warrior like that would have no problem being adopted into any family in any of the villages around here.

"I wish you good journey," he told Jase in halting Spanish.

He smiled at the kid. "I wish you peace."

The boy had had to grow up way too early, way too fast. But with the camp gone and the drug trade pushed back, the villages in the area might be safe at last. Especially if the Don gave up enough information so further strikes could be carried out against his other captains, and against even bigger bosses than him.

Mochi ran back into the forest with one last look at the foreigners, holding the knife as if it were made of gold. Then in the blink of an eye he disappeared, as if the forest had swallowed him.

Jase stood looking at the spot where he'd last stood, then turned and helped the men lift Melanie and the baby up into the chopper. He jumped up after them and settled in next to her, took her hand.

There were tears in her eyes. She kept craning her neck, hoping to catch another glimpse of Mochi.

"How are they?" Jase asked the medic.

"Stable. They'll need a thorough checkup when we get them to the hospital, but I can't see anything that would cause concern." He flashed Jase an impressed look. "I can't believe you made it out of all this alive. I guess there's nothing a man wouldn't do for his family."

His family. The words echoed in Jase's head. He looked at Melanie and the baby, and didn't correct the man.

Epilogue

Rio pulsed with life; spicy scents and music filled the air. She'd instantly loved this dramatic, vibrant city the moment she'd arrived here five years ago. Someday she would move back home to be near her sisters. But not until she finished her work here.

Melanie ran up to her first-floor apartment and unlocked the door. She worked on her housing project only part-time now, but since it was nearing the end, she made tremendous progress every day.

Maria, the babysitter, hurried to greet her. "You have a visitor, *señora*."

And as she stepped forward, she could see Jase sitting at her kitchen table, her son riding on his knee.

Laka, her ten-year-old daughter, was serving them Play-Doh cookies. Her three-legged dog lay across his feet.

The smile Jase gave her took her breath away. God, he looked good. Even better than she'd remembered.

He held her gaze. "I see you've been growing your family."

"This is my daughter, Laka," Melanie introduced the girl. "She has Mochi's smile, doesn't she?" A day hadn't passed in the past six months that she hadn't thought of

Mochi. She'd even sent a care package to the Jesuit mission through the church, with a letter asking the priest to find the boy if he could and pass on her box of goodies.

"There are definite similarities," Jase was saying. "She's probably from the same tribe. How did she get here?"

"Found her when we were surveying the slums for the high-density housing project. She was all alone."

He seemed thoughtful for a second. "Could have been kidnapped by loggers and sold to one of the beggar bosses."

Beggar bosses ran groups of dozens of children, forcing them to beg on the streets in exchange for protection and one measly meal a day.

"She doesn't remember. She's been fending for herself for years. I couldn't leave her there."

"So you adopted her."

She nodded. A single mother of two. Not the way she'd pictured her life, but she was very happy with her two amazing children.

"And the dog?"

"Another slum find." She couldn't help it. Although much older, the dog reminded her of Mochi's puppy. Except this one was missing a hind leg. Not that it slowed her down any.

"Your daughter says you named the dog Chico."

"It's a perfectly good name."

"Your dog is a girl."

So what if *Chico* meant "boy" in Spanish. "She doesn't complain."

Jase shook his head, still grinning, giving her a look that made her a little dizzy.

The baby gurgled and reached for her, and she took

him. Kissed the top of his fuzzy head. "Did you have a good day?"

He smacked his lips.

"He ate well and slept well, *señora,*" Maria said, heading for the door. "See you Monday morning."

"Thank you. Have a good weekend."

Then she was alone with Jase, save the dog and the kids.

He stood. And looked great. Clean-scrubbed, wide-shouldered and a warrior, truly, even in a black T-shirt and blue jeans. A shiny new scar stretched above the eyelid a bullet had nearly ripped off back in that insane fight in the jungle.

"You look good," he told her. "Happy."

"I am. I've grown up some." She'd had time to reevaluate her life; what she had, what she wanted. She knew that she didn't need the attention or validation of others to feel worthy or loved. And she was loved, anyway.

Unconditionally. By her children, by her friends, by her sisters who checked in via the internet almost daily and had flown down twice already to visit.

As for men... Two of the men who worked on the project had asked her out since she'd gotten back. But the truth was, no one compared to Jase.

He was here. Did that mean anything?

"I just got back from an op last night," he said. "My first leave since I last saw you. I missed you."

Her heart fluttered. "I missed you, too."

He smiled.

"Will you stay for dinner?"

"I'd love to."

"When you say you just got in that means..."

"Came here straight from the airport. My luggage

is in the rental car outside. Actually, I would love to use your internet if I could. Haven't had a chance yet to find a hotel."

He was giving her an out, she suspected. In case she wasn't remembering their time together the same way as he did.

They had spent so much time apart already. She didn't want to waste any more by playing needless games.

"You can stay here."

NIGHT HAD SETTLED on the city. Faraway music filtered in through his open window. The children were asleep in their room, the apartment quiet.

Jase lay in his bed, his arms folded under his head, and stared at the ceiling.

He'd told himself that seeing Melanie, making sure that she and her son were all right, would be enough.

It wasn't.

He got out of bed, shrugged into his shorts and padded across the living room. He liked her place: homey and fun, every corner filled with toys, baby paraphernalia all over the place. Not messy, just comfortable, a place where he could see himself spending time and liking it.

The dog came around to investigate, hobbling along cheerfully, tail wagging. Jase scratched behind her ear and patted her. If he hadn't been in love with Melanie already, he would have fallen for her the moment he'd walked into her apartment and seen that dog.

He knocked on her bedroom door.

"Come in."

He opened the door, stepped inside and found himself in the jungle.

Her apartment had a lot of potted plants, but her bedroom took the cake, the walls lined with potted palm trees. More stood on her balcony; the door was open, the balmy night breeze blowing in, playing with the sheer white curtains.

She stood in the middle of the room, as if she'd been on her way somewhere. Her hair tumbled to her shoulders, the moonlight coming from behind her, outlining her figure under the sheer material of her nightgown that fell above her knees.

He gently pushed the dog back out, locked the door then stepped forward. So did she. They met in the middle.

He took her hands and held her gaze. "Hey," he said softly, making sure not to wake the kids.

"You're here," she whispered.

He leaned his forehead against hers. "I've been dreaming about this."

A smile stretched her lips.

He kissed the tip of her nose.

And then he took her mouth.

He meant to take it slow. She wasn't just anyone. She was the woman of his dreams. She was a mother of two, and had all his respect for that. She was someone special.

But when her soft lips settled against his, primal heat washed over him, and all he wanted to do was brand her as his.

He held his desire in check and kissed along the seam of her lips, from corner to corner. Man, he'd missed this.

She opened to him softly, on a sigh, setting his blood on fire.

He tasted her.

Sweet.

Enthralling.

He gathered her closer.

Her hardened nipples pressed against his chest through the thin nightgown. The sensation sent waves of desire through him.

He let go of her hand and set his palms on her slim hips, bunched the sheer silk up, and up and up, then drew the nightgown over her head, just barely breaking the kiss.

Long moments passed while the two of them stood there, skin to skin. He tore himself away at last, when he could, to look at her.

She looked like a jungle goddess in the moonlight, perfect in every way, her full breasts teasing him.

He dipped his head to one of her nipples and sucked it between his lips.

Her fingers dug into his hair.

"Jase," she said on a sigh, as he rolled the nipple between his tongue and the roof of his mouth. He wasn't nearly sated when he switched to the other breast, then back to her mouth again, hooking his hands under her thighs and lifting her.

Her arms folded around his neck as he carried her to the bed, pushing the mosquito netting aside and laying her on the cool, white sheets.

She looked beyond-words lovely, better than any dream could ever be.

He stripped off his shorts before he joined her on the bed, stretching out next to her.

He wanted to extend this moment: the sensation of lying next to her skin-to-skin, the look in her eyes as she held his gaze, the feel of her curves under his fingertips. But hot need pushed him.

He kissed her again, deeper this time, harder. His fingers explored every inch of her body, her neck, her breasts, the flat plain of her stomach, her hips, and the folds between her legs that grew moist at his touch.

She gave herself to him freely, kissing him back, her hands roaming his chest and shoulders. Her unmitigated acceptance humbled him.

He kissed his way down her body, then up again. He slipped his fingers inside her down below, the same time as he slipped his tongue inside her mouth.

She arched her body against his.

He teased her at the same time with his tongue and his fingers, exploring her velvety softness, wanting to make her feel as good as he felt touching her. Her soft moans reverberated in his brain. He wanted her, only her. Forever.

The knowledge that it wasn't likely to happen about killed him. So he pushed it out of his mind and focused only on tonight, only on the here and now, on her sweet, willing body.

When her muscles constricted around his fingers, he swallowed her cries of pleasure.

The need to sink into her was overpowering. But not yet—he didn't want this to be over yet. Not when this night might be the only one he'd ever have with her.

He turned her gently onto her stomach and brushed her hair up and away from her neck, kissed that slim, sexy curve, the outline of the licking flames of her tattoo, then kissed his way down her spine. He scraped his teeth over her firm bottom, kneading her soft skin with his fingers.

She squirmed on the mattress, the sheet bunched in her fists.

"And now I want to hear about that tattoo," he whispered against her skin.

"The last stupid thing I did to rebel against my father." She paused. "He ignored me for most of my life, then after my mom died in an accident at the university lab, he turned into a control freak. Can we talk about him later?" She sounded gratifyingly weak.

"We don't have to talk at all. I'm just going to admire the fine handiwork for a second." Sexy as hell—gave her a touch of the rebel.

When every inch had been kissed, he flipped her again, and pulled up her knees, situated himself between them. Dragged his lips down her inner thigh. Then he tasted her.

And never wanted to stop.

She squirmed against him, her fingers in his hair, whispering his name.

He took his time bringing her to the peak again, his own body near exploding.

He looked up at her as she sailed off into bliss. She wept with pleasure. He nearly wept with need.

He reached for his shorts next to the bed, at last, and pulled a small foil package from the pocket, sheathed himself, then positioned himself at her opening. "Look at me."

She did.

And he entered her, slow inch by slow inch.

Her body felt incredible as it closed around him. He

never wanted the sensation to end. He rocked against her, swallowing a groan of pleasure.

They fit together perfectly, as if her body had been made for him and his made for her. He started with slow strokes, then built speed, losing himself in her. Whatever difficult road had brought him to this point in his life, to this woman, had been worth it.

Pressure built, pleasure swirled, his muscles tightened. They tumbled over the edge together.

They lay side by side, breathing heavily, trying to come to terms with what had just happened.

"You need a man who is steady and true and can be with you every day of the week," he said morosely, sometime later.

"A music teacher," she mumbled against his shoulder.

Jealousy sliced through him. His muscles tightened. A killing rage rose in his belly. "You have someone?"

"I couldn't bring myself to do it. I couldn't stop thinking about you."

He relaxed. They lay silent for a few more minutes.

"The best I can offer is a week or two between missions. You can't settle for something like that. Not with the kids."

She kissed his skin. "Let me decide what we need."

He drew in a deep breath as hope spread through his chest. "I haven't had a steady home since I've been in high school."

"This could be the place. You can come home to us between missions."

"It can't be enough for you. I know it's not enough for me." But it was a hundred times more than he'd dared to hope for before he'd come here.

"It'll be enough for now. You won't work this job forever."

"At least a few more years."

"We'll deal with it like any other military family."

Family.

Sounded right and felt right. He knew beyond a shadow of a doubt that this was what he wanted. "I don't have to be back on base for another two weeks. It'll give me a running start at getting to know the kids." He pulled her on top of him. "During the day. I want to spend my nights making love to you."

She sat up, straddling him, her glorious breasts jutting out in the moonlight. "And when will you sleep?"

"I'm a special ops soldier. I don't need sleep," he scoffed, then gripped her hips and lifted her. He lowered her slowly onto his hardness while he pushed up and inside her soft body.

"I love you," he said.

She gave a teasing smile. "Are you sure it's not just the rescue complex talking?"

"Of all the people I know, you need to be rescued least."

"I know." Her smile grew. "Isn't it great?"

He pushed all the way in, then stilled. "Say it."

She held his gaze, emotions filling her eyes, taking his breath away. "I love you, Jase."

* * * * *

Look for Dana Marton's next book of heart-stopping romantic suspense, THE SPY WORE SPURS,
next month. You can find it wherever
Harlequin Intrigue books are sold!

COMING NEXT MONTH from Harlequin Intrigue®
AVAILABLE JULY 2, 2012

#1359 COLBY ROUNDUP
Colby, TX
Debra Webb
Colby Agency Case #50! Special Colby Agency Companion Guide fan bonus included.

#1360 KADE
The Lawmen of Silver Creek Ranch
Delores Fossen
FBI agent Kade Ryland is stunned to learn he and Agent Bree Winston are the parents of an abandoned newborn, but the problem is—Kade and Bree have never been lovers.

#1361 LIVE AMMO
Big "D" Dads
Joanna Wayne
Faced with insurmountable odds to save her son and herself, Alexis is forced to turn to a sexy cowboy, the last man she ever expected to become her hero.

#1362 COWBOY IN THE CROSSFIRE
Robin Perini
Desperate to protect her young son after he witnesses his uncle's murder, Amanda Hawthorne is forced to seek help from the disgraced Texas sheriff her brother framed.

#1363 BEAR CLAW LAWMAN
Bear Claw Creek Crime Lab
Jessica Andersen
Can a guarded undercover agent and a once burned, twice shy crime-scene analyst find love in the middle of a deadly drug case?

#1364 THE SPY WORE SPURS
Dana Marton
When Grace Cordero saves an injured man in the middle of the night, she doesn't realize that Ryder McKay will soon be taking over her ranch in the name of a top secret mission.

You can find more information on upcoming Harlequin® titles, free excerpts and more at www.Harlequin.com.

HICNM0612

REQUEST YOUR FREE BOOKS!
2 FREE NOVELS PLUS 2 FREE GIFTS!

Harlequin®

INTRIGUE®

BREATHTAKING ROMANTIC SUSPENSE

YES! Please send me 2 FREE Harlequin Intrigue® novels and my 2 FREE gifts (gifts are worth about $10). After receiving them, if I don't wish to receive any more books, I can return the shipping statement marked "cancel." If I don't cancel, I will receive 6 brand-new novels every month and be billed just $4.49 per book in the U.S. or $5.24 per book in Canada. That's a saving of at least 14% off the cover price! It's quite a bargain! Shipping and handling is just 50¢ per book in the U.S. and 75¢ per book in Canada.* I understand that accepting the 2 free books and gifts places me under no obligation to buy anything. I can always return a shipment and cancel at any time. Even if I never buy another book, the two free books and gifts are mine to keep forever.

182/382 HDN FEQ2

Name _____ (PLEASE PRINT) _____

Address _____ Apt. # _____

City _____ State/Prov. _____ Zip/Postal Code _____

Signature (if under 18, a parent or guardian must sign)

Mail to the **Reader Service:**
IN U.S.A.: P.O. Box 1867, Buffalo, NY 14240-1867
IN CANADA: P.O. Box 609, Fort Erie, Ontario L2A 5X3
Not valid for current subscribers to Harlequin Intrigue books.

**Are you a subscriber to Harlequin Intrigue books
and want to receive the larger-print edition?
Call 1-800-873-8635 or visit www.ReaderService.com.**

* Terms and prices subject to change without notice. Prices do not include applicable taxes. Sales tax applicable in N.Y. Canadian residents will be charged applicable taxes. Offer not valid in Quebec. This offer is limited to one order per household. All orders subject to credit approval. Credit or debit balances in a customer's account(s) may be offset by any other outstanding balance owed by or to the customer. Please allow 4 to 6 weeks for delivery. Offer available while quantities last.

Your Privacy—The Reader Service is committed to protecting your privacy. Our Privacy Policy is available online at www.ReaderService.com or upon request from the Reader Service.

We make a portion of our mailing list available to reputable third parties that offer products we believe may interest you. If you prefer that we not exchange your name with third parties, or if you wish to clarify or modify your communication preferences, please visit us at www.ReaderService.com/consumerschoice or write to us at Reader Service Preference Service, P.O. Box 9062, Buffalo, NY 14269. Include your complete name and address.

INTRIGUE

USA TODAY BESTSELLING AUTHOR

B.J. Daniels

**BRINGS READERS
HER HIGHLY ANTICIPATED SEQUEL**

JUSTICE AT CARDWELL RANCH

Six years ago Dana Cardwell found her mother's will in
a cookbook and became sole owner of the Cardwell Ranch
in Big Sky, Montana. Now, happily married and with twins on
the way, Dana is surprised when her siblings, Stacy and Jordan,
show up on the ranch…and trouble isn't too far behind them.
As danger draws closer to the ranch, deputy marshal
Liza Turner quickly realizes that Jordan Cardwell isn't the man
the town made him out to be.

*Catch the thrill October 2 with Harlequin Intrigue®
wherever books are sold!*

www.Harlequin.com

HI69644

*Harlequin Intrigue® presents a new installment
in* USA TODAY *bestselling author
Delores Fossen's miniseries*
THE LAWMEN OF SILVER CREEK RANCH.

Enjoy a sneak peek at KADE.

Kade saw it then. The clear bassinet on rollers, the kind they used in the hospital nursery.

He walked closer and looked inside. There was a baby, and it was likely a girl, since there was a pink blanket snuggled around her. There was also a little pink stretchy cap on her head. She was asleep, but her mouth was puckered as if sucking a bottle.

"What does the baby have to do with this?" Kade asked.

"Everything. Two days ago someone abandoned her in the E.R. waiting room," the doctor explained. "The person left her in an infant carrier next to one of the chairs. We don't know who did that, because we don't have security cameras."

Kade was finally able to release the breath he'd been holding. So this was job related. They'd called him in because he was an FBI agent.

But he immediately rethought that.

"An abandoned baby isn't a federal case," Kade clarified, though Grayson already knew that. Kade reached down and brushed his index finger over a tiny dark curl that peeked out from beneath the cap. "You think she was kidnapped or something?"

When neither the doctor nor Grayson answered, Kade looked back at them. The anger began to boil through him. "Did someone hurt her?"

"No," the doctor quickly answered. "There wasn't a scratch on her. She's perfectly healthy as far as I can tell."

The anger went as quickly as it had come. Kade had handled the worst of cases, but the one thing he couldn't stomach was anyone harming a child.

"I called Grayson as soon as she was found," the doctor went on. "There were no Amber Alerts, no reports of missing newborns. There wasn't a note in her carrier, only a bottle that had no prints, no fibers or anything else to distinguish it."

Kade lifted his hands palms up. "That's a lot of no's. What do you know about her?" Because he was sure this was leading somewhere.

Dr. Mickelson glanced at the baby. "We know she's about three or four days old, which means she was abandoned either the day she was born or shortly after. She's slightly underweight, barely five pounds, but there was no hospital bracelet. We had no other way to identify her, so we ran a DNA test." His explanation stopped cold, and his attention came back to Kade.

So did Grayson's. "Kade, she's yours."

How does Kade react when he finds out the baby is his?

Find out in KADE.
Available this July wherever books are sold.

This summer, celebrate everything Western
with Harlequin® Books!

www.Harlequin.com/Western

Copyright © 2012 by Delores Fossen

Harlequin®

INTRIGUE®

CELEBRATE

DEBRA
WEBB'S

50th COLBY TITLE WITH A
SPECIAL BONUS SHORT STORY!

Colby Roundup, the story of one woman's
determination to remember her past before time
runs out, marks Debra Webb's 50th Colby title,
and to celebrate Harlequin Intrigue® is giving you
a special BONUS Colby companion short story
included with this book!

*The excitement begins July 2
wherever books are sold!*

www.Harlequin.com

HI69626

SPECIAL EDITION

Life, Love and Family

USA TODAY bestselling author

Leanne Banks

begins a heartwarming new miniseries

Royal Babies

When princess Pippa Devereaux learns that the mother of Texas tycoon and longtime business rival Nic Lafitte is terminally ill she secretly goes against her family's wishes and helps Nic fulfill his mother's dying wish. Nic is awed by Pippa's kindness and quickly finds himself falling for her. But can their love break their long-standing family feud?

THE PRINCESS AND THE OUTLAW

Available July 2012!

Wherever books are sold.

This summer, celebrate everything Western with Harlequin® Books!

www.Harlequin.com/Western

HSE65680

Looking for a great Western read?

Harlequin Books has just the thing!

A Cowboy for Every Mood

Look for the Stetson flash
on all Western titles this summer!

Pick up a cowboy book
by some of your favorite authors:

Vicki Lewis Thompson
B.J. Daniels
Patricia Thayer
Cathy McDavid

And many more...

Available wherever books are sold.

Saddle up with Harlequin® and visit
www.Harlequin.com

ACFEM0612